MIDNIGHTS LIKE THIS

BOOK CLUB BOYS
BOOK 2

MAX WALKER

Edited By: ONE LOVE EDITING

SYNOPSIS

Eric Ruiz

I never thought I'd see him again.

We ended things on a horrible note, and it was all my fault. So when I bump into Colton at a local coffee shop, I'm convinced it's some kind of prank.

But it wasn't. Colton was back in town, and he needed help. His mom was killed in a burglary gone wrong, and he's convinced there's more to the story.

He's also convinced I'm the only one who could help him. It would require being fake boyfriends and going with him to his family retreat, but at least we had some real experience being together.

Shouldn't be too hard, right?

Colton Cooper

I always wondered if we'd meet again.

Eric was my first love. Even though we had to keep it a secret, he had held my entire heart.

And ended up breaking it.

But when I see him again after all these years, those feelings come rushing back. Along with an idea.

Eric had a lot to make up for. So the least he could do was fly with me to the South of France and try to figure out who in my family was responsible for my mom's death.

I just hoped history didn't repeat itself.

LETTER TO THE READER

Hello!

And thank you for picking up this book. You're reading the special illustrated paperback edition, with a cover created by an incredibly talented illustrator. This book was an absolute joy to write and I hope it's the same to read.

<3
Max

ALSO BY MAX WALKER

The Hammerhead Heist

The Gold Brothers

Hummingbird Heartbreak

Velvet Midnight

Heart of Summer

Audiobooks:

Find them all on Audible.

Christmas Stories:

Daddy Kissing Santa Claus

Daddy, It's Cold Outside

Deck the Halls

———

Receive access to a bundle of my **free stories** by signing up for my newsletter!

Tap here to sign up for my newsletter.

Be sure to connect with me on Instagram and TikTok **@maxwalkerwrites.**

Want more Max? Join Max After Dark.

Max Walker

Max@MaxWalkerWrites.com

1

COLTON COOPER

THE SOUND of a shattering champagne glass mixed with an ear-splitting cry. Time seemed to still. Paused, as if someone had pressed a button on the remote. The air in the spacious living room grew as heavy as lead, sinking into my lungs. It mixed with the adrenaline and elation that came from solving the case.

But at what cost?

Eric looked at me, big brown eyes swirling with a storm of pain. I wanted to reach out, grab his hand in mine. I wanted him to tell me that it would be okay. That the plan worked. It was all worth it... or was it? Did I just lose more than I'd gained?

That's when my brother spoke, breaking the thick silence. "I didn't do it. I didn't kill my mother."

Archie's voice was hoarse, his throat constricting with the panic that no doubt flooded through him. Jen, my sister, held back tears, a shaking hand covering her mouth.

My entire body felt like it had been struck by lightning. Every single cell in my body was fried from the shock.

Eric had laid it all out for us. He'd listed the exact reasons why my brother would be motivated to end our mother's life. It all made a twisted, sick kind of sense. I didn't want to believe a single word of what Eric was saying, but deep down, I knew he only spoke facts.

"You don't even belong here, on this trip." My brother advanced toward Eric, pushing aside the love seat that his wife sat on as if it were made of paper. She shouted again, grabbing onto the armrests. I'd never seen my brother this angry before, his face a cherry red and his hands forming tight fists. "You and Colton concocted this entire plan to, what, frame me? Do you want me off the will, Colton? More money for you and your fake boyfriend? Huh? Eric, do you get a cut?"

My eyes opened wide, as if my little brother had slapped me across the face. I shook my head, trying to process it all. My dad was dead silent as he stood by the window, watching us all as if he was seeing us for the first time in his entire life.

"Eric and I are..." I looked at him. The man I loved. The man I used to love. The man I'd brought here under fake pretenses, the man I'd been unable to deny real feelings for.

Was I losing him tonight, too?

"Colton brought me here as a detective, first and foremost. Yes. Our relationship was fake, but the information I uncovered is all real, and I wouldn't have found any of it if I didn't act the part with Colt," Eric said, speaking the truth and stabbing me directly in the chest while he did it.

Shit... That hurt. Maybe it was because emotions were already sky-fucking-high, but hearing Eric say that he came here just as a detective made my chest tighten even more than it already was. Like an invisible boa constrictor was intent on squeezing every last molecule of air I held in my lungs. I looked out the window at the dark and cloudless sky, wondering how the hell this trip had turned tits up in a matter of minutes. And was it all my fault? Should I have left it all alone? Should I have never invited Eric? Never have come up with this wild plan in the first place? I could see now that all the roads led to heartbreak. Each and every single one of them.

Because, no matter what, at the end of the day, my mom was still dead, and my "fake boyfriend" was now accusing one of my brothers of her murder.

How did that not amount to heartbreak of the worst kind?

"This is fucking crazy," Kendall said, pushing past my grandma, who looked like she was two seconds away from passing out onto her girlfriend. "We're standing here, dressed like fucking Clue characters, talking about Archie like he could hurt a fly, much less our own *mother*. Do you see how ridiculous that sounds?"

Eric took out his phone, opening it to a video that took up his entire screen.

"What is that?" Archie asked, trying to snatch the phone from Eric's hand but proving to be too slow.

"It's proof of your involvement in Amelia's death."

The room fell into a pit of silence and dread. Eric turned to me, that teddy-bear look of his twisted in pain. "Do you want to stay here for this?" he asked me.

I nodded, unable to speak.

Eric pressed Play, and the sounds of my mom being strangled to death filled the room, making me regret my decision to stay, along with every single fucking decision in my life that had led me up to this nightmare come true.

2

COLTON COOPER

Three Weeks Earlier

A MUG FELL to the floor, shattering in thick chunks of porcelain. "Ah crap, sorry," the student said as she adjusted her backpack. The barista came around the counter with a smile and a hand broom, telling her not to worry about it as he swept up the mess.

The coffee shop was starting to fill up with people now that the university classes had let out, and the kids were filing in for their shots of espressos and macchiatos that would help them get through whatever studying or exams they had coming up. I rarely came around this side of town, but it was my sister's favorite spot, and I could never say no to her. Since we were tiny kids barreling through the house, being chased by our four other brothers, she was always my best friend, my buddy, the one that had my back, and I had hers.

So if she wanted to come to this trendy little spot to

talk about our mother's suspicious death before we flew out to our annual family retreat, then so be it. I'd entertain her.

"What'd you get?" she asked, swirling her cup of mostly sugar and a dash of coffee. Ice clinked inside, her lips shining around the straw as she took a sip.

"Just a regular coffee. Two sugars."

"You're sick. A sick, sick man. I don't know how you can drink that motor oil."

"Jen, it's really not that bad. And it won't throw me into a diabetic coma like your bucket of whip cream and cinnamon."

"You know me. I love coffee. I just also *hate* coffee. I'm complicated like that."

I shook my head, smiling. A group of backpack-carrying kids dropped into the bean bags next to our table, their bags unzipping and their laughter and chatter filling the air.

"Are you all packed?" Jen asked.

"We've still got two weeks before we leave—of course I'm not packed. Are you?"

"We have two weeks left before we leave—of course I'm packed. Do you understand the logistics it takes to make all this happen?" She threw her curly black locks over her shoulder and winked. I rolled my eyes, although I couldn't deny that my buzz cut and very anemic skin-care routine paled in comparison to the regime Jen went through each day. "I also have a lot of mental preparation to undergo for the shitshow that's waiting for us, so the less I have to worry about before the trip, the better."

I huffed out a breath. "Shitshow is an understatement."

"It's going to be the first time we're all together since it happened."

"I know... I know."

"Have you talked to Matt? Archie? Kendall?"

All siblings, none of them as close to me as Jen. "Only through text, and nothing important. They all seem to be just fine, judging by their social media posts, but we all know that filtered smiles can only go so far."

"Yeah, it's all bullshit. Archie hates his wife, Matt hates his job, Kendall hates herself. And I hate all of them. Crazy how that works, huh?"

"You know who didn't hate them? Mom."

"Not true. Did you already forget her blowing up on Archie for marrying someone she thought would ruin the family name she worked *so* hard to build up?"

"Yeah, but they got over that, and Archie turned into her favorite kid."

Jen shot me a skeptical look. "And yet Archie wasn't even at her funeral. What a joke."

"He didn't even have a good excuse."

"Nope. Then again, neither did Matt. He was off backpacking through Thailand. At least he sent flowers, though."

"Orchids. Mom hated orchids. She loved lavender."

Jen chuckled. "She sure did hate orchids." She looked out the window, shaking her head. "Something happened to her, Colt. Something bad. I just know it. Down in my bones, I know someone hurt her."

Maybe that's what made Jen and I so close. We always worked our way through this world on the same wavelength. Her feelings were mine, and mine were hers. We understood each other on a level that ran soul-deep. A look between us could carry a hundred questions, another look carrying the accompanying answers. Our inside jokes were numerous, and our secrets were kept tight, locked in the vaults of our lifelong friendship.

One secret that was recently deposited into the vault was something that felt difficult to admit, even to myself, in the quiet spaces of my thoughts. How could anyone be okay with thinking their mom was murdered? The woman who'd brought them into this world, the one who'd worked tirelessly and thanklessly to dig her family out of poverty and give them a life that many people can only ever dream of. She'd amassed a fortune while doing her best to support the children she did it all for.

And now she was dead. A robbery gone wrong. As if any robbery can ever go right.

"What if it really was someone trying to rob her?" I asked, already knowing the answer.

"Oh, someone definitely tried to rob her, but I'm sure it was the inheritance they were after. Not the jewelry or the clothes or the cars."

Jen's statement sent a chill down my spine. Her implication was clear but hard to swallow. Our mom had built up a fortune, and with that blessing came a massive curse. Money changed people, but not just the ones who were earning it. When the bank account was as large as my mother's, it created a kind of gravitational pull that affected how people in her orbit acted. Cousins thrice removed would crawl out of the woodwork after her Forbes article came out. Old friends from high school that she couldn't pick out of a lineup appeared at her front door, begging for a handout. Employees and neighbors and dog walkers and randoms off the street. They all wanted a slice of the pie.

A lot of us stood to gain a life-changing amount of money from my mom's death, and that sent up red flags all across the board. It was Jen who brought it up first, mentioning how maybe money could have been a motivating factor.

Then came the details of her death. Details that didn't exactly add up. She was murdered in her own home, strangled to death and left to die on her brand-new Persian rug. The police said the robber must have forced his way in, and when my mother didn't relent, she was choked out.

Except there wasn't any sign of a break-in. And my mother wouldn't have opened the door for just anyone. She'd always warned us: if anyone ever came after us for something, we gave it to them. Material possessions could be replaced, but people couldn't. She was a cautious woman, with security cameras all around her house.

Cameras that happened to be down for maintenance — a total of fifteen minutes. That's all the time it took for someone to strangle our mother and take some of her more expensive pieces of jewelry before running out and leaving behind a shattered family.

It didn't add up. And now we were set to all get

together at our family villa in France for a yearly vacation that appeared to be on the precipice of getting canceled until my father had announced that he was selling the villa and that this would be our last year to visit. He wanted us there, enticing the family further by saying the will would be read at the villa.

And so here we were, a few weeks out from flying overseas to spend time with someone who'd murdered our mother, discussing the prospect in a coffee shop without having any inclination of what to do first.

I tried to rub the tension out of my forehead. "I think I need another coffee," I said, finishing the last bit that was left in my cup. "Want anything?"

Jen swirled her half-full cup and shook her head. She leaned back in her chair and looked out the window, the overcast sunshine casting a soft glow on her, reminding me a lot of Mom. They shared the same sharp cheekbones and thin nose, the same long dark hair that had skipped my genes altogether. My short blonde hair came directly from my dad, along with my slightly shorter and much stockier frame, built even more by the years of rugby I played in college.

Six years separated me from my last match, and although I still went to the gym, I had lost some of the definition I'd had back then. Which I was completely fine with, and none of the guys I'd hooked up with had complained, either.

That made my mind wander as I stood in line behind a couple of frat bros chatting about their next social. I looked around the coffee shop, wondering if there were any older and more sensible guys I could check out. My taste wasn't exactly picky, but I did like my guys to have some chest hair and, at the minimum, a total of five brain cells.

No one. I was about to turn my focus back to the colorful menu that hung above the smiling baristas when a familiar face jumped out at me, having just walked in.

An *extremely* familiar face, and one I hadn't seen in years. Not since we were both in the police academy together. I dropped out a few months into it, but that was more than long enough for me to get to know the man currently walking toward me, shocked amusement playing on his handsomely bearded face, shaved around the neck and kept trimmed around his face.

He looked just like the guy I had spent all those nights with, pretending to be brushing up on our laws and call codes only to be brushing up on each other, tracing secret words between our shoulders and on our lower backs. All night long. Sometimes throughout the day, too. We were fire and gasoline, opposites that created a guaranteed chemical explosion, one of those explosions burning us to a crisp and destroying anything we had between us.

I was gone a week after our fight.

"Eric," I said, holding out a hand, Eric returning it with a genuine smile on his face. He still had that same teddy-bear kind of grin, the one that disarmed anyone in a five-foot vicinity. It was a superpower, and one I'd seen him use during my brief time in the academy. He had a knack for getting past people's defenses and effortlessly extracting information he knew was vital. From where we stood, my sister was blocked from view, so she couldn't see how completely dumbstruck I was by this random meeting.

And that's when an idea hit me—as out of the blue as this meeting was. It struck like lightning and glued me to the floor, making me miss whatever Eric had just said as my brain tried to put together the pieces of thought shrapnel, forming a crazier and wilder idea with each passing millisecond.

And one that could possibly work.

3

ERIC RUIZ

NO FUCKING WAY.

I could hardly believe it. Colton Cooper. The boy with the golden-brown hair and the electric and unforgettable smile. I'd died a thousand deaths at the tips of his fingers, brought back to life each and every time by the voltage behind those lips. We'd spent countless nights exploring each other, veiled in a thin curtain of shadows and secrets. We weren't supposed to be together, not in the way we wanted to. We were best friends in the academy, and everyone saw the camaraderie between us as clear as the winter sun.

And I'm sure many of them saw the underpinnings of that friendship. Colton being out and proud at the time only made things harder for me. It muddied waters that were already full of shark-attracting chum. I'd expected my inner desires to be laid bare at any moment, ripped apart by the circling predators: my parents, my grandfather, my high school friends, my televangelist aunt.

None of them would have supported me, and as a momma's boy who strived to make everyone around him proud, that made things difficult.

Too hard, too risky. I cut things off with Colton on a night I'd never forget. Thunder boomed louder than my heart, which rattled so hard against my ribs I was sure I bruised a couple. Colton's blue eyes caught the lightning strikes, throwing them back at me, brighter through the tears that formed.

He dropped out of the academy a week later and stopped answering my calls.

"I—hey," I said, finding that Colton hadn't lost an ounce of that electric magnetism he'd had at nineteen. If anything, it had only grown stronger, refined by a powerful jaw and a perfectly lined-up and trimmed beard.

Damn. He somehow managed to get hotter.

I tried not to think about the way I must have changed since he'd last seen me.

"You're looking great," he said, as if plucking my insecurities directly from my head and crushing them under his boot.

"You too," I volleyed back. "Are you visiting?" The only thing I knew about Colton was that he'd moved back home—Los Angeles, where his mother owned a multimillion-dollar media empire. We didn't follow each other on social media, so his life had been effectively hidden from my own for years now.

He looked happy, so I guessed that was a good thing.

He still had the same ear-to-ear grin and perfectly messed-up head of blond hair that would always earn him a comment from the administrator, who'd had a not-so-secret crush on him.

He chuckled, shook his head. He ran a hand through his hair— a ringless hand. Not that I was looking or anything.

"Moved here a couple months ago, actually. There's been some big life changes that had me picking up my shit and hunting for something new but familiar. My sister's been here for years, so it only made sense I came back. I felt like my time here was cut way too short."

"Well, welcome back to Atlanta." I matched his smile, even though a slight awkwardness clung to us like smoke from a recently extinguished fire. Funny how life worked like that. You could find the most comfortable, most intimate moments of your life with someone— we shared nights of not just sex but of baring the deepest parts of ourselves to each other, our most daunting fears and our biggest, most lofty-headed dreams, all while holding each other, naked, fingers trailing across every curve and every ridge, playing with patches of soft hair and squeezing on the firmer parts.

And then, with that same exact person, you could find yourself standing—fully clothed—in a random coffee shop, wondering if saying a quick goodbye would just make everything easier.

"Life changes, huh?" I asked, deciding not to take the easy route. Not just yet.

"Yeah." Colton nodded, the smile wiping away with a sigh. "It's our mom. She passed this year and left the family in complete shambles."

"Oh, Colt, I'm so sorry. Amelia was always so nice to me that day she dropped you off at the academy. I remember she stayed behind to help me unpack all my shit, even though your side of the room was all set up already."

His eyes flicked out to the street, a muscle in his jaw twitching as the stress climbed through his body like a physical force. Colton was always a feeler. His emotions were as big as the rings that circled Saturn and just as complex. He was never very scared to show them, either. It was something I admired about him.

There was a lot I used to admire about Colton, actually, and all of it was flooding back to me as I stood a couple of feet away from him, being reminded of what a great guy he'd been and what a huge idiot I'd been, possibly making one of the biggest mistakes of my life. I hated to live with regrets and tried to keep as little of them as possible, but I'd be a bold-faced liar if I said I'd never thought about Colton, wondered where he was and how he was doing.

Guess I just had to wait to find out.

"She was super mom, alright. Always wanted to treat everyone else like they were her own kids."

"What happened?" I asked, moving to the side so a group of students could pick up their coffee orders. The buzz of the blender filled the air, mixing with the relaxing soundtrack filtering out through invisible speakers.

"A botched robbery. Killed in her own house."

My eyebrows jerked halfway up my face. "Oh no, fuck. Did they catch the killer?"

Colton shook his head. He crossed his arms, the twitch in his jaw getting more apparent, like he was grinding down on the inside of his cheek. This time, it wasn't from sadness, though. Anger sparked in those ocean-blue eyes, turning the waters into a reflection of a darkening storm.

"It doesn't even add up, Eric. She had cameras all around her house that conveniently go down for fifteen minutes, the same fifteen minutes someone entered her home, where they took about a half-million worth of jewelry before strangling my mother."

"Strangling?"

"She was found with strangulation wounds all across her neck. It wasn't like the burglar saw her, panicked, and grabbed a vase or a knife. My mom may not have even seen the person. They hunted her, strangled her from behind, and left her there so that my brother could find her an hour later."

That didn't sound like a regular break-in, if there ever was such a thing. Someone robbing a home usually did their homework. They studied the occupants, knowing which home likely had the most valuable things to grab and when it would be empty. Colton's mom had more than a million in jewelry on just her person alone, so to grab only half that amount during a time when the robber could run away with the entire bank... it didn't make much sense.

Unless there was a bigger prize.

"Was there a will?" I asked, following the thread.

"Of course there was. None of us have read it yet or even know what's on it. A lawyer's been going through it with my father. It'll be read at our family retreat in a few weeks, which will *definitely* be interesting." Colton cocked his head. "Why do you ask?"

"Because your mother was worth an astronomical fortune, and sometimes that amount of money can attract some bloodthirsty souls."

"So you're still just as sharp as you were in the academy, huh?" The way Colton spoke made me think he had the same feelings I did. "It's hard to consider the idea that someone in our own family could have done this, but it's not exactly like we're all saints, either. And now we're set to be under the same roof for two weeks, with the shadow of our mom's death following us around. Which makes it a perfect opportunity to figure out what really happened to her."

I arched a brow and examined the hard-set lines of Colton's expression. It was a mixture of determination and hope.

"Are you still a cop?" Colton asked, the shift in conversation surprising me.

"No, I left the force a few years ago. I've got my own PI business now. It's small, but I've got pretty consistent work."

"A private detective, huh?" Colton's smile grew, his eyes lighting up an entire shade brighter. "That makes my next question even more relevant."

"And what's that?"

Colton's next question came completely out of the blue. "Would you be down to come and help me figure out who killed my mom?"

4

COLTON COOPER

I COULD TELL my question knocked Eric off his orbit. He wasn't expecting that, but then again, I wasn't expecting a random meeting with one of the only people I felt was capable of helping. Eric had a bloodhound's snout for clues and cases, cracking situations that seemed destined to go cold, and he'd do it effortlessly.

And that was at the very start of his career, when even the higher-ups at the academy were floored by his detective skills. He'd be in the break room, chatting it up with me and eavesdropping on the cops a table over, leaving the break room by offering them a case-solving suggestion. It was wild to witness and something I'd never forgotten about him. Not that there was much about Eric I could forget.

"I know it's a big ask," I said, speaking over a particularly rowdy group of patrons. I shot a look over at the corner where my sister sat, blocked from view by a jutting wall. "My sister and I know that something happened to our mom, and we think the answer is going to be at the chateau."

"Chateau?"

"Yeah, this year's retreat is in the South of France."

Eric nearly tipped over.

"I'll pay for your flight," I offered with a smile. "Listen, you know how big I am on fate and signs. You walking into this coffee shop today feels like one of the biggest signs of my life. Neon and flashing."

"And how am I going to explain why I'm there? I doubt your family is going to be happy with someone investigating them for murder."

Okay, good. He was considering it. The part of me that was scared he'd laugh in my face and walk off was slowly quieting down. Not that Eric would have ever done that to me, but then again, it had been years since we'd last spoken—people change in much less time than that.

"You can be my plus-one."

Eric cocked his head.

"Fake plus-one, obviously."

He cocked it in the other direction.

"It's not like we don't have the practice," I said, breaking through some of the thick ice that had formed around our feet. Eric blinked at me, as if trying to blink through the shock. I smiled a little wider. I'd always liked catching Eric off guard. He was cute when he looked a little shaken.

"I—well, I mean, that's not a lie."

"No," I said, shaking my head. "It's not. So what do

you think? Want to take a business-deductible trip with your new fake boyfriend who just so happens to be your old fake boyfriend?"

"We weren't fake boyfriends back then."

"So you call us sneaking around and only hooking up behind closed doors a real relationship?"

"Did you want to hook up with the doors open?"

I slanted my grin and narrowed my gaze. "You know what I mean."

He chuckled, the sound throwing me back to the first days I'd heard that sound. Soft and light, bubbly almost. I'd fallen hard for Eric's laughter and his big brown eyes and his furry chest and his thick—

"I have to check my schedule," he answered. His eyes bounced between mine as if he were searching for something. Maybe trying to see if this was all some kind of dumb joke. "I do want to help you, though, Colt. If someone is responsible for your mother's death, then I want to be the one to find them and put them behind bars."

"Okay, go open up your Google calendar and get back to me. And I'm serious about the *fake* part of my plan, Eric. This isn't a ploy to try and get back with you. You made it very clear that we were never going to work out. Besides, I'm talking to someone now anyway." The words still stung, even though I was the one saying it this time. Memories of that stormy night came shooting back to me. Flashes of tears and lightning, amplified by the pain that reached out from my chest, like tendrils growing out from my heart and choking off the rest of my body. I had fallen hard for Eric back then, in only a month of knowing him. I had already pictured an entire future with him. The two out-and-proud gay cops on the force, saving lives and coming home together at the end of the day.

It was a silly little dream, made by my silly little heart over some silly little feelings.

I wasn't going to make that same mistake again, even if Eric wasn't in the closet anymore (which he wasn't, judging by the posts on his Instagram from a pride parade... not that I was checking up on him or anything).

"Colt, I have a lot to say about that night. Most of it revolves around the words 'I'm so fucking sorry.'"

I put my hands up as if I was about to bat away his apologies. "No need. It was over three years ago. I've moved on, and I'm sure you have, too. So it'll make this fake-boyfriend thing even easier."

"Here, have my number and send me the dates for the trip. I'll get back to you before the end of the day."

We traded numbers, except when Eric put his into my phone, his full name popped up. It was the same number. I could have called him at any point during these last few years, but then what would I have said? *Hey, I think you broke my heart beyond repair, and yet I still can't stop thinking about you... what's up?*

"How's things in Eric-ville been?" I asked as he tucked his phone back into the pocket of his jeans. They were rolled at the ankle so that his colorful blue-and-yellow socks were showing.

"It's been... well, pretty wild, actually. It's a long

story, but basically, one of my best friends was being stalked and ended up being kidnapped. I helped rescue him and his fiancé."

It was my turn to get knocked off my orbit. "Holy fuck, seriously? When was this?"

"A few months ago. Thankfully, no one was hurt. Well, besides the stalker, who got a bullet to the shoulder as a souvenir for all his troubles."

I arched a brow and shook my head. Aside from Eric's investigative skills, he also had excellent shooting skills, which undoubtedly came into play when he was saving his friend. "Damn," I said, "And here I was thinking you were going to tell me you settled down behind a white picket fence and opened up a bakery or something."

"Nope, no fences for me. I live in a high-rise," he said with a wink.

I chuckled at that, wondering briefly if that apartment was shared with anyone.

Just then, the barista called out that Eric's online order was ready. He turned and went over to the counter, giving me a moment to appreciate the way he filled in his jeans. Eric had always had a body that made my core light up and my briefs tighten. He was tall and built like a sturdy bear—broad shoulders with a juicy chest and thick thighs that could easily crush my head between them. He was just my type—if only he hadn't already broken my heart into a million little pieces.

Damn.

Eric smiled as he took a sip of his coffee, his soft

brown eyes settling on mine. The warm light from the cafe made them glow like they'd been sprinkled with golden glitter.

Damn, damn, damn.

"Alright, well, it was great seeing you, Colt. Really."

I scratched the back of my neck, suddenly wondering how I could prolong this chance meeting, but before I could invite Eric to come sit with my sister and me, he said, "I've got to get going. I've got a book club meeting to prepare for tonight."

"A book club, huh? So maybe that white picket fence thing wasn't too far off?"

He laughed and took another sip of his coffee, his top lip coming back coated in whip cream, which he quickly licked off. "That book club was what got my white picket fence shot up. We all got involved with helping find Noah's stalker while also getting drunk and reading great books."

"It sounds like a fun time."

"It is," Eric said, flashing his pearly whites. "You know, we're starting a new book this week. Want to join in? It would be a good way for you to connect with some people in Atlanta. And you always loved to read—you had that closet full of books."

"I joked it was the only reason why I couldn't stay in the closet, because my books didn't leave me any room. I'll have you know I've gotten a bookshelf since then." I puffed out my chest and acted proud of my evolution, dusting off some invisible dirt from my shoulder. "That does sound like a great time. Minus the stalker part... I'd love to join."

"Good, perfect. I'll text you all the details, then."

I went to shake goodbye, but Eric moved in for a hug, arms wide. I took it gladly. Eric's arms wrapped around me tight, and I got a good whiff of his oaky cologne, making that spring in my core tighten even further. I was half-tempted to kiss him on the cheek, feigning some European influence from a recent trip to Italy, but managed to hold myself back.

"Where did you disappear to?" Jen asked as I sat back down at our table. My sister threw a curious look around the corner of the wall she sat behind, but Eric was long gone. "I was about to call the cops and report a missing person."

"I was making a business call."

Jen pursed her lips and gave me a sisterly glare. She knew damn well I was lying but didn't pursue it any further. We went back to discussing the matter at hand, except my mind continued to replay that chance meeting over and over and over again.

5

ERIC RUIZ

THERE WAS no way I could help Colton.

My schedule was packed, and beyond that, I just wasn't sure if I was mentally prepared to handle being in a fake relationship with the one I felt got away. Especially not now that I was out and honest with myself. Back then, I was able to blunt some of the pain by lying, by telling myself it didn't matter if Colton was out of my life because we would just never work out together. It was a deep and festering denial that corrupted almost all aspects of my life and made me push away the man that had been able to effortlessly make me happy on a daily basis.

But I wasn't in the closet anymore, which meant there'd be no protecting myself if I caught feelings during our professional arrangement. And Colton seemed to have moved on from our fiery flings, having mentioned he was already seeing someone.

Why did that bother me so much?

I washed up the last of the dishes that were in the sink and went over to the fridge, where I grabbed a beer and popped it open. With the chores done and the house clean, all I had to do now was wait an hour or two for the first people to show up. That gave me some time to go over the book we were starting today called *A Family Affair*, about a dead body being found on a cruise ship, where a family reunion was being held for a woman's eightieth birthday party.

I slumped down on the couch and reached for the book on the coffee table but grabbed my laptop instead. I kicked my feet up on the mint-green stool and took a swig of my IPA before clicking into my internet browser and setting the cursor on the address bar.

That's where I typed in Amelia Cooper.

An image of Colton's mother popped up on the screen, attached to a Wikipedia page. She wore a violet business suit as she stood in front of the blurred-out logo of her company. Her smile was sharp and her eyes even sharper, a sapphire blue that seemed to cut through the screen and drill right through me. I remembered that intensity, but I remembered her warmth and kindness much more.

If I couldn't make it to Colton's family trip, then maybe I could still help from afar. If I kept him an arm's length away, then maybe I could keep my feelings protected and solve this case all at the same time.

News articles about Amelia's death were some of the first links to pop up under the search. None of the articles were particularly lengthy or illuminating. They all said the same thing: multimillion-dollar media mogul found dead in her home after a botched robbery. There were mentions of her businesses and business partners, along with talk of how her wealth would be split up amongst her large family. A couple of articles pointed to her charitable work and painted a picture of a woman who gave as much as she received. It was all benign information that didn't give anything to the suspicions that this was a possible murder.

Until I landed on one particular website that looked as if it had been created during the first dot-com boom. It was called Who's Eating the Rich, advertised by a bold red-and-white banner that flashed every time my mouse scrolled over it. The black and sparkling background with the pixelated header and brightly colored links was giving very much Angelfire vibes.

But I wasn't there for the website designer's information. It was the brief but juicy article filling my screen that interested me.

The header read Amelia Cooper, killed in cold blood for massive inheritance.

I skimmed through it at first, trying to extract the things that jumped out at me most based off instinct alone. Words like *disowned, furious, prostitute, thief* all screamed out at me. It looked like Colton's family was as tangled a web as any, with Colton's estranged brother landing in jail for aggravated assault and robbery, only to come out with his record somehow expunged and a cushy new job at his mother's company. Except this article was insinuating that the brother—Archie was his name—still wasn't happy with the handouts his mother gave him. He wanted more, which was proven by a series of slightly unhinged tweets shot off at three thirty in the morning where Archie went on a rant about how little he was being paid and how he needed to start a GoFundMe if he wanted to make his rent for the month.

A quick search showed me that those tweets were nowhere to be found, which meant they were either deleted or fabricated. I'd have to ask Colton about them when he came over for the book club—

Not that I was working his case. It wasn't the smart thing to do. I had five other cases I was working through and had zero mental or emotional capacity to take on a possible relationship, regardless of how fake or real it was meant to be. And *especially* not with Colton.

A knock on my door drew my attention. I shut the laptop and set my beer on the glass coffee table with a clink. I walked past my air freshener just as it sprayed a fresh mist of lavender and honey. The first of the Reading Under the Rainbow crew smiled at me under a mane of freshly done curly hair, her book and a notebook held to her chest.

"Yvette, how are you," I asked as I pulled her in for a tight hug. I could smell the strawberry from whatever hair products she had used to get her curls so shiny and bouncy.

"Ugh, I've been better. Work was *wild* today."

"Well, come in and let me get you some champagne. That should cancel out whatever crap happened at work."

"I like your math," she said, slipping off her sandals and coming inside. She followed me into the kitchen, where I grabbed a baby pink bottle of rosé and popped off the cork. The sound of more knocks mixed with the bubbly fizz of the champagne being poured into glasses. I grabbed an extra one and set it on the counter before Yvette took over pouring duties so I could go open the door.

"Tristan," I said with a smile, pulling one of my closest friends into a hug. He appeared to have come straight from a kickball game, wearing his team's blue-and-yellow jersey with grass-stained white shorts. "Good game?"

"Nah, we lost by a pretty big amount. But we still had fun, so whatever. I didn't have time to change, though."

"That's fine," I said, closing the door behind him. "As long as you don't smell like you were running around with a bunch of sweaty guys and their balls, then I won't complain."

"Don't catch me on a Sunday, then," Tristan said, shooting me a wink.

"Or Saturday, or Monday, or Tuesday," I shot back with a smirk.

Tristan rolled his eyes. "That was a particularly slutty week for me. I had no idea I'd end up hooking up with five guys. I think it was because my Saturn was rising or something."

"Yeah, something was rising alright."

Tristan scoffed out a laugh before Yvette walked out of the kitchen with three flutes of champagne in her hand. "You boys are gross," she said, holding out the hand with the two glasses. Tristan and I grabbed one each.

"You heard all that?" Tristan asked.

"Of course I did. Eric lives in a two-bedroom apartment, not a countryside villa."

We went to the couch, where we settled in to wait for the rest of the gang. We were only missing four more, plus Colton, who I was equal parts nervous and excited to hang out with. Sure, I wasn't taking his case, but that didn't mean I couldn't have him around my orbit from time to time. And I really did want to help him get settled into his new home with a good group of friends, even if that meant I'd be putting myself directly in front of Cupid's line of fire.

My phone buzzed on my lap. I flipped it over and read Colton's name, figuring he was asking for the address to my place again. Instead, I was greeted with an apology and a long-winded explanation about having to cancel on tonight's book club meeting.

"What? What bad news did you just get?" Tristan asked.

"Huh?" I looked up from my phone, not realizing I was that transparent.

"You look like you just read a puppy's obituary with the way your smile dropped."

I huffed out a breath and typed out a quick response to Colton, letting him know it was totally fine that he couldn't make it to the book club. Outside, a clap of thunder boomed somewhere off in the distance.

"Remember that new book club attendee I emailed

everyone about? Colton? He just texted me to say he couldn't make it."

"Ah, gotcha," she said. She took a sip of her bubbling champagne, her eyes narrowing from behind the rim of her glass.

"Is this the same guy you fell in love with back in the police academy and stopped talking to because you were scared of being yourself?" Tristan asked as nonchalantly as if he were asking what we were having for dinner.

I nearly did a spit take but was able to swallow down my drink before I sprayed it all over my best friend. "I, uhm, I've already talked about him?"

"Yup," Tristan said, an arm thrown on the back of the couch and his feet propped up on the stool.

"I do faintly remember you mentioning that story," Yvette said. "That's wild how you guys bumped into each other again after all those years."

"It is— what's even wilder is that he asked me to help him with a case. And it would require us having to be fake boyfriends so I can attend his family trip to France."

Tristan's jaw dropped, and Yvette made a jumbled mix of sounds.

"And?" Tristan asked when he finally recovered from the shock of my reveal. "Are you going to take the case?"

"Absolutely." The pair lit up, smiling wide. "Not. No, I can't put myself in that position. He's moved on, and I still feel guilty about how it all ended. How am I expected to go and hold his hand in one of the most romantic places in the world without catching feelings again?"

"Would it be so bad if you did?" Yvette asked.

"Yes, considering he said he's with someone."

"So how are you going to be fake boyfriends? Wouldn't the family know about the other one?" Tristan pointed out before taking a big swig of his rosé.

"Maybe the family doesn't know about the other one yet," I said with a shrug.

"Then it must not be all that serious." Tristan arched a brow, Yvette nodding her approval. These two weren't helping the situation at all. Why were they poking all these holes into my carefully crafted excuses?

Our conversation was put on indefinite hold as more knocks announced the last of the arrivals. Tia and Jess were standing next to Jake and Noah, the four of them looking like the brochure of a Pride parade with Noah's rainbow shirt and Tia's rainbow shoes practically glowing under the hallway lights.

I let my friends in, grabbing the tray of freshly baked fudge brownies from Jess, the scent of them already making my mouth water.

"What's up, guys?" Noah asked as he sat down on the love seat.

"Oh, nothing," Tristan said. "Just talking about how Eric is seconds away from agreeing to a trip to France with his future fake husband."

That was the moment our entire book club night devolved into an attempt at getting me to say yes to the fake-boyfriend mess.

And by the end of the night, I had to admit they were getting me pretty close.

6

COLTON COOPER

TONIGHT WAS a royal fucking hot mess.

It wasn't supposed to be. I had planned on attending Eric's book club and making some new friends before I was set to spend the night with Shane, the guy I'd been talking to recently. He wanted to watch a recent release on Netflix—which I had assumed meant we'd be dealing with a whole different kind of release by the end of the night.

So imagine how surprised I was when Shane texted me saying he wanted to talk. We didn't even get to the "boom-boom" intro for the movie before Shane was telling me he had to cut things off.

"Are you serious?" I asked him, standing in his barely furnished living room, looking at his unshaven face and expecting a loud laugh any second now. Shane didn't have the best sense of humor, but even for him, this was a pretty dumb joke.

"It's not a joke."

Oh.

"Seriously?" I echoed. "Why? We were planning a trip to Disney just yesterday."

"I know— that's mainly why. I've gotten a little too connected with you. You're a great guy, Colt. A catch, hands down, no cap." He played with the rounded tongue of his hat, flipping it backward. "But I've already got a boyfriend. Fiancé, actually. He's been deployed this entire time. He comes back next week, and I don't want our relationship to get ruined."

My jaw dropped as my head fell forward. "You have a whole-ass fiancé fighting somewhere overseas, and you have the balls to sleep over at my house nearly every night?"

"He's a doctor, actually, but—"

"I don't give a fuck if he's Cher. You're an asshole."

"If it makes you feel better, I wasn't with anyone else. Just you."

I huffed out a disbelieving breath. Lightning crackled overhead, bathing his living room in a bright white light. "Yeah, just me and your soon-to-be husband. Jesus. I should have known. I should have realized you were talking to someone with all those text messages you'd send." I winced, hating how quickly I had fallen for this big-dicked douche bag. It seemed like every guy before him was a dud, so when we'd stayed up to see the sunrise on our first date, lying naked and spent in his bed after a night of some of the best sex of my life, I really felt like I'd found someone who was boyfriend material. Beyond the sexual chemistry, the conversation between us was always fun and sometimes even enlightening. Shane had studied history in college and always had some kind of interesting fact to spill, connecting past with present.

Too bad there'd be no more future. Not between us.

"Does your fiancé know?" I asked, already assuming the answer.

"No, he doesn't. And I'd really appreciate it if you didn't say anything to him. We've fooled around before but never got into something as serious as you and I got."

I shook my head, the disgust rising in me like bile. He even *said* it. Admitted that we were serious, more so than any of his other flings from the past. And what if his fiancé hadn't been coming home for another year? Would I have been strung along the entire time, developing stronger and stronger feelings, until Shane grabbed the knife and plunged it through my ribs? Thankfully we'd only been dating for a few weeks, so it wasn't like I wasted tons of time on this douche, but it still fucking sucked.

Another crack of lightning sounded from overhead. I took the keys out of my pocket and turned toward the door, trying not to focus on the disappointment and hurt that had started to creep through my chest. I had gotten my hopes up. Let myself fall for a fantasy that was just that: a fantasy. Something reserved for the pages of a book, not for the real world.

"I'm really sorry, Colton. If I were single, things would be different."

"Yeah. I'm really sorry, too. For ever swiping right on you."

Shane ran a hand through his messy brown hair, his expression turning pained. "Don't say that. I'd never consider you a regret."

"So you think considering me as a side piece is any better?" I could feel the temperature in the room rising. My self-worth was taking a hit, alongside my heart and my ego. What was it about me that made every single fucking guy in my life use me like a wet rag, tossing me to the side when they were done with me? Why couldn't I find a man who wanted me as badly as I wanted him? Someone I could trust wholeheartedly, who I could share memories with and travel the world with and not have to worry about.

"Maybe you can meet Dixon? Maybe if all three of us get along—"

"Even if I was open to the idea of a throuple, do you genuinely think I'd want to do it with you? After what you're putting me through?" I laughed, the sound coming out like a hyena cackle. "No fucking way."

I didn't want to hear any more. Shane said all he had to say, and I was left to deal with it on my own. I'd dealt with much worse; this would likely only suck for a few days, but that still didn't blunt the way I currently felt. With my shoulders slumped and my tail between my legs, I left Shane's apartment for the last time, deciding I was done with men for the foreseeable future. Maybe it was time I focused on myself. Maybe I needed to guard my heart a little better than I'd done in the past.

Outside, the rain was coming down in sheets. Wind rattled a nearby street sign that looked like it was five seconds away from taking flight. I had parked on the street across from his building, so I put an arm over my head and ran for it, jumping over a puddle and into another one before I reached the car.

I got in, rain streaking down my face, my shirt and shorts soaked after that brief jog through the rain. I wiped it off with the back of my hand and took out my phone. My heart raced. Thunder roared from the storm that only appeared to be getting stronger, the sky blotted out by ink-dark clouds that were only visible when lightning struck.

I opened my contacts and called the one person I had on my mind, the one person who always knew what to say when life was messy.

The phone rang and rang and rang. No one answered, like I expected. The voicemail prompt came on before the beep sounded.

"Hi, Mom." Instantly, my voice began to crack. "I miss you." I looked ahead, wondering if the blur in my vision was from the rain on the windshield or the tears in my eyes. "I could really use some of your famous pick-me-ups right now. I'm having some boy trouble and don't know what to do to fix it. I remember you telling me to value my heart more than my heart's desires, and that really stuck with me. I'm trying to put myself first, but I can't help it. I *want* to be with someone. I want to share my life with someone special. I just can't find that special someone."

The voicemail message cut me off, telling me it had

gone on long enough. I let my head drop against the head-rest and gripped the steering wheel tight.

Life didn't seem fair, not in the slightest. Here I was, in a brand-new city, a few weeks away from flying off to a scenic chateau so I could spend the days with my mom's potential killer, and I'd just been broken up with. That wasn't even taking into account the bump-in I'd had with none other than Eric Ruiz, the first man who had broken my heart and also one of the only men I felt could help me figure out who'd killed my mom.

Nah, none of this shit seemed fair, but then again, what the hell had I done to deserve a smooth ride through life? Sure, I tried to be a good person and always made sure to never leave anyone hurt in my wake, but that didn't mean I automatically earned a drama-free pass. As nice as that sounded, I also realized how unrealistic it was.

No. I'd have to deal with this shit one way or another.

I unlocked my phone again and called someone else. This time, I expected them to answer like they always did.

"Halleloo," my sister sang on the other end of the line. "What's up, Colt?"

"Hey, Jen. I'm going through it tonight. That guy I was talking to just cut things off with me—apparently, he has a fiancé overseas that's coming back next week or some shit."

"No... oh, Colt. Damn it. I'm sorry."

"It's fine," I said in a way that made it clear it wasn't

very fine at all. "Do you still have that bottle of pinot your boss gave you?"

"The vintage one I got for Christmas? Hell yeah I do. Come over and we'll pop it open. I'll put on a dumb movie and make some slightly burnt popcorn, just how you like it."

"You're the best, Jen."

She chuckled. "And you're sociopathic for eating popcorn like that. I'll see you in a little bit."

"See you soon," I said, hanging up and feeling a little better. It would take way more than crispy popcorn and some good wine to get over this, but at least it was a start.

No more guys. None. Never.

An image of Eric's smiling face flashed across my mind.

Well... maybe not never.

7

ERIC RUIZ

I WAS GOING to help him.

That was the thought that first popped into my head the morning after our extremely derailed book club night, where my friends all set aside their books and focused instead of convincing me I had to take Colton's case. They all had valid points and well-balanced arguments, but it was Noah who clinched it at the end.

"Just imagine it was one of us who needed your help," he had said, Jake nodding at his side on the couch. "Colton was one of your best friends, and now he needs your help. Just based off that alone, I think it's an easy decision."

He was right. Colton and I may have had a tangled history, but at the root of it all, we had been incredible friends. It was what made it so easy for me to fall for him, and what scared me the most about falling for him. I knew that with how strong our connection was, we'd never be able to hide our relationship, and as a closeted young kid suffering under the heel of toxic masculinity, I just wasn't ready for that.

But I had come a long way as a twenty-eight-year-old man who was out and proud and who'd now wear heels when he occasionally dressed up in drag. Being gay didn't scare me anymore, not like it had back then.

I stretched out underneath my comforter, realizing there was another reason why I had to say yes: so I could say sorry.

My excuses might have been valid, but that didn't take away from the pain I'd inflicted back then. I'd never forget Colton's face as I told him I'd never love him. I may as well have kicked him in the nuts and spat in his face. He didn't deserve that. Not Colton, who had one of the biggest hearts I knew.

That's not the only thing about him that's big, either.

More images flashed across my sleep-fogged brain. Nights of body-melting passion that spilled over into the mornings, watching as the sky slowly changed color outside of the bedroom window, Colton tangled up in my arms, gently stroking me while I kissed his forehead.

My bedsheet tented at the memory, my morning wood throbbing. I pushed the sheets down and opened my legs, closing my eyes as I took myself in a loose fist.

Colton was the first guy I'd ever been with. It all started one night after a mutual friend threw a keg-filled birthday party. We went back to our apartment and stayed up in the living room, talking about all kinds of random shit. At some point, our knees were touching, and I noticed Colton's hands going to his crotch, as if he were readjusting.

I was the one who made the first move. I leaned over and kissed him, missing his lips and getting his cheek instead. He had smiled, asked what I was doing. I said I was just being drunk and stupid. Colton replied by kissing me back, whispering against my lips, "Let's keep being drunk and stupid, then."

I came four times that night. It wasn't just that Colton's body was perfectly chiseled from his time at the gym, or the way he would suck my cock without any restraint, or how he'd jerk us both off in one hand until I was covered in cum—there was something far deeper between us that made our sex so explosive. And the seed of that connection was still lying dormant somewhere in my chest, having sparked back to life after the encounter at the coffee shop. I knew there was nothing I could do about it, considering the fact that Colton had clearly moved on, but I also couldn't deny it existed.

Still, I'd have to ignore it for now. Good thing I had somewhere else to focus my attention.

I closed my eyes and stroked, up and down, feeling the velvety soft heat from my shaft make my palm warm. I grabbed my tightening balls, massaging them. My toes curled. I stretched my legs, flexing the thighs, feeling a mixture of pure pleasure and desire. As much as I enjoyed my own hand, I couldn't stop thinking about how good it'd feel if it was Colton's hand.

Or mouth or ass.

"Fuck," I hissed out into my empty bedroom. I was

getting close. Nearly there. I quickened my strokes, tightening my grip. I used my leaking precum as lube, spreading it on myself, imagining the wet sensation coming from Colton's lips instead. He'd always had a way with his tongue. I'd be unraveled before he even got me into his mouth.

My alarm started to blare. I'd usually wake up before my alarm went off whenever I had a lot on my mind, and today had been one of those days.

I rolled over, my erection pressing into the mattress as I reached for my phone to turn off my alarm. Instantly, my screen was filled with notifications and emails. I was going to set it back down and finish jerking off when one subject line snagged my attention.

RE: Question about your blog post on the murder of Amelia Cooper.

Before going to sleep last night and once I decided I was taking up Colton's case, I had sent an email to the author of that one blog post that seemed to have a lot of information on the family. I wasn't expecting much of a response, and especially not one so soon, but there it was.

She'd agreed to a chat with me. She said she'd be free in the next few hours for a Zoom call but flat out stated she couldn't give out more information than what was in the post. Which was fine—I figured I could try and pull something useful out of here before the call was over. I typed up a quick response and set a time for later in the day to talk with her.

Woosh. The sound of the email sending came through the speakers. I set my phone back, glad to have at least one lead to follow before leaving for France. The article seemed very thorough and well detailed with information that should have been sealed in a police report and not handed out to the general public. She'd mentioned the exact items that were taken, along with the discovery of a long blond hair, which couldn't be DNA matched to anyone in the database. These were things that she either had to have been told (and if so, by who?), or she somehow discovered it all herself.

Regardless of what had happened, I wanted to know. But in the meantime, there was something else a little more pressing at hand.

I laid my head on the pillow, rubbing my chest and belly before going back to my stiff length. Two more minutes of fantasizing about Colton bouncing on my cock was all I needed. I blew, spraying my load all over my stomach, coming to a fantasy that I was sure would remain as just that. A fantasy.

Well, and a memory.

———

"HI, Vicky. Thanks for setting aside some time to chat with me."

"Totally fine," Vicky said, her audio coming through with a little static. She was sitting in front of a tall but largely empty bookshelf, wearing a white shirt that blended into the white and barren bookshelf. She had a sharp cat eye painted on and an even sharper smile that seemed to cut through the computer screen. "You're interested in Amelia Cooper's death, right?"

"I am. I'm working on a case and stumbled on your article. You seem to know a lot about what happened that day."

"It was one of my weirder posts. I normally am a little more vague with what I write, especially because I don't want to hamper any kind of investigation, but this one was different. It seemed like the cops were writing it off as a robbery, but I'm not so sure about that, so I shared everything I knew." She lifted a mug—one of those souvenir boob mugs with a Vegas tattoo—and took a sip. I blinked, and she looked down at the mug, chuckling. "It's my son's. He thought it was funny."

I briefly wondered if there would be as big a market for mugs made to look like dicks but pushed myself back on track. I'd have to figure out my *Shark Tank* pitch at some other time.

"And how did you come across the details? I couldn't find anything online with the type of information you were able to get."

She cocked her head and arched a well-shaped brow. "Now, now, you know I can't give up my sources like that."

Ah, so there was a source.

"No need for specifics. I just want to know if it was someone involved directly with the family."

"That's sounding awfully specific to me," she said, clearing her throat. "Whoever it was came to me because they wanted the truth. That's really all I can say."

"Which means they likely think there was foul play here."

She shrugged and drank from her mug again.

"Was there anything said that you didn't include in the article? Anything at all?"

Vicky seemed to dig through her thoughts, her tongue prodding at the inside of her cheek. A baby cried from somewhere off-screen. Her eyes darted to the left before coming back to the camera. "I was told that there was a camera that wasn't offline. She had a secret nanny camera in the living room that filmed what happened, but the cops weren't able to find it."

"Interesting," I said, leaning back. That only further proved the theory that this was a targeted attack and not a random burglary. Someone had to have known she had that camera hidden away, but who would she tell?

The screeching grew louder. Vicky closed her eyes and rubbed the bridge of her nose. "Sorry, Theo gets very cranky if he doesn't get fed around this time. I've got to go. I know I haven't really given you much to go off, but all I've got is what I was told. I'm just the messenger here. That's all I am."

"Thank you, Vicky. You've been extremely helpful."

"If I think of anything else, I'll call you."

"Perfect. Thanks again."

She smiled and lifted her boob mug up in a cheers before clicking out of the chat.

I closed the computer and went for my phone, wanting to break the good news to Colton. He'd be happy to hear that not only was I taking on the case but that I already had a decent trail of bread crumbs I wanted to follow. Someone in his family seemed eager to speak to Vicky and to get all this information out there, and the tidbit on a secret camera could come in handy. Not only did it prove the fact that whoever was behind this had intimate knowledge of Amelia's life, but it also meant that somewhere out there, there was video evidence of what had actually happened.

Colton picked up on the second ring. He sounded out of breath and explained he was just wrapping up at the gym.

Guess his love for working out never left him. He had tried to get me into a gym, but it never clicked for me. I found other ways to stay healthy, enjoying a long walk or bike ride down the Silver Comet trail.

"Colt, I've got some good news."

He cut me off. "Wait, before you say anything, I just want to let you know... forget about it. About my mom's case... It was a dumb idea. I'm not even going on the family trip, so just forget it."

8

COLTON COOPER

WE WERE BACK in the coffee shop after Eric convinced me to meet with him in person. I wasn't budging over the phone, so he must have thought he'd have a better chance of convincing me if he were sitting across from me. It was a Sunday morning, so the place wasn't as busy as it was when we first bumped into each other.

I took a drink of my caramel Frappuccino and leaned back, shaking my head. "I just don't think it's a good idea anymore," I said, explaining myself to a still-bewildered-looking Eric. He wore a black baseball cap flipped backward, so a curl of shiny black hair swooped down onto his forehead.

My damn kryptonite.

Dick-tonite?

Dick... tonight was my kryptonite. Alright, I was onto something. But I'd have to share my genius wordplay with Eric some other time, when he wasn't looking like a damn snack on wheels.

"And why not? You seemed pretty enthusiastic about it just a couple days ago," he said, one arm thrown casually on the back of his chair. The buzz and whir of the coffee grinder directly behind us made me speak up a little louder.

"Yeah, a couple days ago, before I was reminded again why men suck worse than taxes and death." I rolled my eyes and took another sip of the sugary drink. "I don't think it's a good idea for me to be in a relationship right now. Even if it was a fake one."

"Did something happen with you and your boyfriend?"

I swallowed down a gulp. Scratched at the back of my neck. Looked up at the beige ceiling speckled with white dots, wondering how the hell I managed to end up sitting across my first-ever heartbreak while he asked me about my most recent heartbreak.

"My boyfriend was kind enough to let me know he had a fiancé overseas. So it's safe to say we aren't boyfriends anymore."

"Ah fuck, I'm sorry, Colt. That's... fuck."

"My thoughts exactly."

He looked genuinely upset on my behalf, which was... well, kind of cute. Damn it. That just made me think the 'fake-boyfriend' idea was dead-on-arrival. I thought I was done with all of Eric's wit and charm, but clearly, he still had some kind of effect on me. I couldn't imagine what would happen if we were made to hold hands and kiss, regardless of the theatrics behind it.

And then there was the nagging thought that maybe I was overreacting over my mother's death. Not that any reaction to a parent's passing should be considered as an "overreaction," but after some serious soul-searching last night (and an entire bottle of wine), I realized that maybe my emotions had gotten the best of me. Jen and I became riled up and concocted an entire theory based around a couple of facts.

"Whatever," I said, taking in a deep breath. "It's just not worth it. Besides, I think maybe what the police said happened is the truth. Why should I go and play Sherlock Holmes when all my mother deserves is to rest in peace."

"Because *I* also don't think what the police are saying is the full story."

I chewed on my bottom lip as I looked into Eric's soft brown eyes.

"I found something out this morning, before I called you. Your mother had a nanny cam that was online at the time of the murder, and it should have caught the whole thing. But it wasn't recovered in the search. Someone knew about the camera and took it with them before they left. It makes me think that whoever did this must have known your mom very well. Did you even know about the nanny camera?"

The walls of the coffee shop felt like they'd been blown to smithereens, leaving me in an open-air cafe with my ears ringing. I blinked, the pale yellow walls covered in colorful art prints still standing. "No, I had no idea. Do you know where it was hidden?"

"No, I wasn't able to get that."

"How'd you find this out?" I asked, sorting through the possible meanings of this seemingly massive discovery.

"I called the author of this blog post. She's got a lot of inside information, which makes me think someone in your family or very close to it is the person leaking this information. Could be someone in the force, but you know cops hate talking to reporters."

Shit. "This changes things."

Eric nodded his head, agreeing. "Let me help you, Colt. I think I can get to the bottom of this."

"You were always such a top, though," I quipped, the words flying from my mouth before I could even put thought behind them.

He chuckled. His tan face caught a pink glow as he looked out the window, the quiet Atlanta street only now just beginning to fill up with cars as people went off to brunch with friends or church with family.

"So you really think someone might have murdered my mom for some reason other than a few stolen necklaces?"

He turned back to face me. His expression answered before his words did. "I do."

I thought the most I'd have to worry about this week was a profit-and-loss sheet I had to pull together at work. Little did I know that my week would end in a bombshell revelation that left me with no choice but to go back to my original idea.

"Fine," I said, determination making my chest puff up and my shoulders stiffen. I had to do this for my mom. If someone in our own family had taken her life, then I wouldn't rest until they were caught and punished. "Let's do it."

Eric perked up, a smile crossing his face, framed by a five-o'clock shadow that seemed to be more than a few hours early. "I promise I'm going to try and figure this one out. And we won't cross any lines. We'll take this fake relationship however far it is you feel comfortable."

"And that's not very far," I said, deciding to be honest and up-front with him. "I'm really not ready for anything right now, and considering what our history is, I think it's important we set up boundaries. Plus sleep with a pillow between us at all times."

"Good idea," Eric said, although I couldn't help but detect what sounded like the shadow of disappointment in his tone.

"I'm glad your detective skills haven't gone anywhere. I can't believe you were able to put this all together in the span of twenty-four hours. That's impressive."

Sure, we were far from cracking the mystery behind my mother's death, but this was the closest I'd felt hope ever since she died. My instincts about Eric were right. He had proven himself someone who could squeeze answers out of a rock.

"There's still a lot more to be done, but at least we're on the right track. I'm going to need a rundown on the rest of your family at some point. Everyone who's going to be at the chateau and maybe even the ones that won't. The more I know, the better prepared I can be." Eric was clicking into detective mode right in front of my eyes, leaning forward on the table so that his thick forearms drew my attention before I forced my gaze back up to his glowing brown eyes. He had long, butterfly-like lashes that nearly barreled me over every time he blinked.

"I'll write up a Cooper family guide for you when I get home." I glanced at my watch, surprised at how much time had already gone by. Eric always had that special ability around me: speeding up time like some kind of handsome superhero. "Shit, I've got to meet Jen in an hour." I rose from my seat, feeling slightly more okay with this wild plan I'd come up with. Eric and I would just have to set down some rules and lay down a couple of boundaries, and I would just have to stop wondering how those lips would feel kissing me or how his big hands would feel wrapped around my hard cock again.

"Let's meet up tonight for dinner," Eric said as we stood up, our chairs creaking in the quiet coffee shop. "That way, we can have a proper catch-up."

"Sounds good to me. Plus, we need to get our story lined up if we want my family to believe we're together."

"Thankfully, we've already got some building blocks to work off of."

I chuckled, following him out to the street. "Yeah, thankfully."

9

ERIC RUIZ

WHY WAS I NERVOUS?

I spent most of my afternoon pacing crop circles into my carpet, wondering how this would all play out, my mind buzzing with "what ifs" and "should I's." I took an hour-long steaming hot shower, which usually helped to unclog any brain folds that may have been blocked up, but even with the scalding hot water and clouds of steam, I still couldn't fully decide if this was a good idea or not. Should I have offered to take Colton's case without the stipulation of us having to be fake boyfriends? Maybe I could have worked it from here while he went to the family reunion and fed me whatever information he found useful?

But that part of me was much smaller than the part that was excited to be next to Colton again, regardless of what rules had been set in place between us. He had been one of my best friends back then, and even if we could just get back a quarter of that magic between us, then I'd be happy.

First, I had to figure out what to wear. I grabbed a baby blue and white plaid shirt that always seemed to net me some compliments, tugging on a pair of dark jeans and switching out my watch band for a dusty-blue one. It took me a minute in the bathroom to tame my unruly herd of cowlicks, completing the entire look with a silver necklace and a spritz of Tom Ford cologne.

"There," I said, glancing at myself in the bathroom mirror. I'd been appreciating how I looked lately, especially as I pushed up against my early thirties and simultaneously developing a no-fucks-given attitude. As a bigger guy, I'd dealt with a lot of bullshit in my life, especially coming from the sometimes six-pack-obsessed headless torsos on the Grindr grid. There was an unnatural—even unattainable—standard for gay men and their bodies, pushed forward by the need to present as some kind of Greek god in order to be accepted, even though my body was just as worthy of worship as someone with biceps and pecs.

It was dumb, and I was glad to be at a stage in my life where I just didn't care. You either took me and my love handles, or you didn't. Fuck you, I'm having fun.

That was my motto, and I was sticking to it.

I locked up my apartment and walked down the hall toward the elevator bay, passing by my new neighbor, Steven. He was a quiet guy but always offered a friendly wave, and he'd introduced himself the first night he moved in, which I thought was sweet. He'd asked about joining the gay kickball league after seeing my shirt, saying he was looking to try and make a couple of friends. I let him know the details and also brought his name up at the book club, where everyone agreed an invite was totally fine.

"Oh, Steven, before you go, I wanted to let you know about a book club my friends and I have. It's called Reading Under the Rainbow. We read mostly mysteries and thrillers and get drunk and play games. Want to join? Our next meeting is on Monday."

Steven's eyebrows rose in mild surprise, his lips rising with them in a smile. "Oh, that sounds so fun. I think I should be able to make it." He moved the bags he was holding from one hand to another. It appeared to be a bunch of stuff from the pet store. I could see fish food from the top of one of the bags.

"Perfect. I'll text you the details."

I could tell his arms were tired from the number of bags he was carrying, so I let him go, waving as he went down the hall and disappeared into his apartment.

Reese Witherspoon was going to have to watch out if our book club kept growing at this rate.

I got into the elevator and felt the butterflies stir up again. They didn't settle down for the entire fifteen-minute drive to the restaurant, which consisted of me blasting Bad Bunny and only hyping myself up even more.

As I parked my car in the restaurant's parking lot, I realized just why I was feeling so nervous. This was a date. Maybe not an official one, but a "fake" one at the very least, and that was way more than we'd ever had back when we were secretly together. I couldn't even imagine going out in public as just us two—my fear of being linked together would have been too strong.

Fuck... I wish I could turn back time.

Unfortunately, that was something not even the all-powerful Cher could do, so I was stuck with the past and had to focus instead on the future. That was something I could at least attempt to affect.

"Hey there, Eric." I turned just before entering the restaurant, spotting Colton getting up from a bench previously hidden by a perfectly manicured hedge made to look like a model's posed hand. The restaurant we were at was called the Grove, and it was famous for the floral art installations and excellent food.

"Hey, handsome." I couldn't help it—Colton was more than handsome. He looked like a high-end fashion model with his fresh haircut and sharp navy blue sports jacket, making his tan watch and belt pop against the white T-shirt, French-tucked into a pair of slick blue pants.

"I wasn't sure what the dress code was here," he said, and I detected a slight pink color entering his cheeks.

"I'm pretty sure you nailed whatever the dress code is." I opened the door for him. We entered the waiting area, which was covered from floor to ceiling in vibrant green plants. The hostess station was made to look like the stump of a tree, and it sat under the tendrils of a rose-covered ivy.

We gawked at the rest of the restaurant as we were

led to our table, set against a window that looked out to a colorful garden lit up by different-colored hues, the lights changing periodically and creating different effects with the otherwise still foliage.

It was stunning, and yet I couldn't quite take my eyes off Colton, who popped against the wall of purple lavender behind him.

Not a date, not a date, this is not a date.

"Great choice," he said, settling into the red leather seat and grabbing the menu.

"It's been on my radar for a bit. Figured tonight would be the perfect night to check it out."

The waiter came by, a smiley guy with a curly mustache and a couple of visible tattoos of different insects, and took our drink order, complimenting Colton on how fresh his haircut looked. Colton gave him a wink and a thanks before cracking his knuckles and settling his eyes back on mine.

"Well, looks like we won't be needing to ask for refills tonight. I've got a feeling he'll keep a close eye on us," I said, smirking at Colton.

He brushed my comment off with another laugh before setting aside the menu, his blue eyes digging a hole directly through my core. "So, should we talk about the case?" Colton asked. An air of business came over him as he sat back, face set in a stern and unreadable look. I tried to decipher those stormy blue orbs as best I could but couldn't crack the code.

Colton used to be so easy to read for me. I would be able to tell his mood through a simple grunt or headshake.

Now, with years separating us, I could barely even tell if he was happy or not to be here.

"Give me another day or two to get things together on the case. Tonight, I think it should be about us." I decided it was best if I clicked into business mode with him. We had work to do, as special as all of this felt. At the end of the day, we were together to help figure out what really happened to Amelia. *That* was my top priority, and I couldn't let anything—or anyone—distract me from that.

"Before we show up at the chateau," I continued, "we need to be on the same page about everything. I have to know the ins and outs of your family. Plus, it'll help with the case."

The waiter cut in with our drinks and a freshly baked bread basket, pouring a full glass of pinot noir for me and giving Colton his Juniper Junebug cocktail, a sparkly neon pink drink with a dragon fruit perched on the rim of the glass.

"Cheers," Colton said, raising his glass and clinking it against mine. "To us reconnecting."

"Cheers to that."

I took a healthy swig from my glass, swirling it as I set it down. I reached for a warm piece of bread as Colton sorted out his thoughts.

"Where should I even start? My family's compli-cated, like most of them. We've had some major blowouts, but we've also had some of the best moments of my life together. Like when my sister Jen came out as trans at our Christmas party and everyone rushed to the tree to throw out the old gift labels and replace them with her new name. Or the time me and all—well, most—of my siblings went on a family trip to Bali. It was wild and spiritual and so fucking fun. My family has moments like those that give me a lot of pride to be a Cooper.

"But there's also a lot of skeletons in the Cooper closet. My brother's drug addiction and gambling problem nearly tore us all apart, and that's only scratching the surface, really."

"This is Archie?" I asked, recalling his brother's name from all those nights we had stayed up talking. He was having issues even back then. Colton had been so worried about him he couldn't sleep one night, not until he got the call that his brother was at home and okay.

"Yup," he said. "He's turned everything around, though. Dropped the drugs and the gambling. He picked up coding. Now he's got a steady and really well-paying job with a wife who seems to really love him, so I'm happy for him."

I set a little mental sticky note next to Archie. I'd have to look into him a little deeper.

"Speaking of relationships, do you think anyone is going to question if you show up with a new guy to the South of France?"

Colton shook his head and waved off my concern. "My family is pretty nosy and interconnected, but I've been keeping to myself lately, so it wouldn't be a surprise if I showed up with a guy. We'll say we've been together for two months. That sound okay?"

I nodded, taking a bite of the buttery bread, following it with a sip of my red wine before a counterthought hit me. "Although, I wonder if two months is a little too soon to be taking me on a family trip? That might seem fishy."

"Hmm, you're right. Let's settle on six months, then. That's half a year. I've done crazier things."

"I feel like we're haggling here. Two months, no four, alright six, and we've got a deal."

Colton chuckled, his lips curling into a smile as he drank his bright pink concoction. "Okay, so six months. And where'd we meet?" he asked.

"Let's keep it simple: online."

Colton cocked his head. "I think we can get a little more creative than that."

"Listen, the more creative we get, the more chances we have at messing up. We want everyone on this trip to feel completely at ease, with as little of their guards up as possible. No one can suspect something's up with me being there, so our story *has* to stay consistent."

"Okay, okay. Online it is. But Tinder, not Grindr. We have to class it up a bit."

I scrunched my brows at that. "There's plenty of strong relationships that come out of Grindr. My last long-term relationship was from there."

"And where are they now?"

I went to debate Colton but realized it was a moot point. He shot me that casual wink of his that instantly lit my core on fire. "I'm joking," he said. "I know Grindr is more than just anonymous cruising, but still, my experiences haven't been all that great. Like, there was this one time—nah, forget it."

"What? What were you about to say? I think fake

boyfriends need to know everything about each other, even hookup nightmare stories."

Colton laughed and rubbed at the back of his neck. "I showed up and he was wearing a furry suit, which, fine, I'm not yucking anyone's yum, but he gave me *no* heads-up—or paws up? Whatever, you get what I mean."

The conversation veered off track after that as we discussed our worst Grindr hookups, commiserating over some wild experiences and enjoying our time together, this fake date feeling awfully real by the end of it.

10

COLTON COOPER

GOD DAMN IT.

This was a date.

Realization dawned on me sometime between my fourth and fifth Juniper Junebug drink. Those damn pink love potions were doing a number on my inhibitions, and I found myself leaning forward and staring wistfully into Eric's eyes on one too many occasions. He had a way of wrapping me into his storytelling that was effortless. It didn't hurt that the man was a walking Renaissance painting. All bold lines and color and raw emotion. I could look at him for hours and still keep finding something new to appreciate about him.

And then I remembered the heartbreak I'd just been through, along with the heartbreak the man sitting across from me had put me through, and my walls instinctively shot back up. I couldn't let myself catch feelings all over again. I wasn't ready for that yet, and besides, there was plenty of other fish in the sea that didn't have the title of "original heartbreaker" next to their name.

"That was great," Eric said as he pocketed the receipt. I tried getting my card in the waiter's hand, but Eric was much faster, nearly knocking over a half-drank glass of champagne in his haste to pay.

"It really was," I said, rubbing my satiated belly and smiling across the table. "We didn't really talk about what we needed to, though."

"Nope," Eric replied. His eyes narrowed, smile widening. "So what do you say about taking this to a bar? There's a chill one nearby. We can go over the case there."

I chewed the inside of my cheek, mulling over the invite. Spending more time with Eric sounded equal parts dangerous and alluring. I definitely wanted to talk about the case, but I knew doing that at a bar was only inviting trouble. We weren't even "officially" fake boyfriends yet, and I was already fawning over Eric like a lovestruck schoolgirl. What was going to happen when we had to hold hands and play the part in front of my family?

"No," I said, setting the napkin on the table and moving to stand. "Sorry, Eric. I just think I might need the night to myself. I'm pretty exhausted."

Eric looked crestfallen. As if I'd just denied him a ticket to see his favorite artist front row and center.

I wonder if that's still Imagine Dragons?

I'd have to ask him. Knowing your partner's favorite

band was probably important, but the question would have to wait.

"You sure?" he asked. "The trip is in five days—we don't have much time. I want to capitalize on every second."

Shit. The trip really was coming up, and there was still plenty to discuss between us.

But still... storm clouds clapped with lightning and thunder inside my head, bringing me back to that painful night when the man I had loved told me he could never do the same for me. Maybe I should have been over it— I *thought* I was over it— but standing only a couple of feet away from Eric threw me right back to that night. It was the darkest moment of my life and led me down some even darker roads. My thoughts were all broken and shattered, the pain becoming too difficult to bear. Thankfully, I had Jen to console me and drag me out of the depths of my darkest thoughts, but it still didn't heal without leaving a scar.

And he still hasn't even apologized.

"I don't know..." I said, glancing at my watch as if I had somewhere important to be at eight o'clock at night on a Sunday.

"Come on. I'll buy you one drink, and then we'll bounce. I just want to go over who I need to keep my eye on."

"Fine. One drink," I relented, rolling my neck and feeling the pops in my spine and along my shoulders. "*Maybe* two."

"Let's go, Junebug."

I hiccuped, a wisp of the Juniper Junebug pool I had formed in my gut escaping me. "Please don't call me that." The room spun a little more than I had expected it to as we walked out of the restaurant, the emerald-green plants appearing to dance on the walls as I went past them.

"Where we headed?" I asked as I pulled out my phone to call an Uber.

"It's called Blake's, but we can walk from here. It's a nice night, and it's not too far."

I pocketed my phone and followed as Eric started down the street. He was right—it was a beautiful spring night, with only a couple of fluffy clouds drifting across the darkening night sky and a gentle breeze that stirred the trees, just now getting their color and leaves back after a particularly harsh winter.

"I'm glad you're back, you know," Eric said as we were stopped at a crosswalk, the red light from the street-lamp shining down on his face. "I really wish we had stayed in touch. I just felt... like such a fucking asshole. And that feeling never went away. I knew I couldn't reach out to you; I knew I had to wait for you first. So I waited, and I waited."

"I would have been fine with you reaching out, just for the record."

He looked at me with those big brown eyes of his, an entire universe worth of riveting stories waiting to be told, and yet no apology anywhere in sight.

Just. Say. Sorry.

"I'm—" Before he could get the words out, we turned

a corner and bumped into the short line leading up to the bouncer at the bar. He dug for his wallet and pulled out his ID. A part of me—the one that wasn't walled off from emotion—that part of me felt a small fiery-hot ember of anger. I was getting frustrated with Eric again, and we weren't even a day into our fake relationship yet. He was never that great with speaking his emotions, but I blamed that on the toxically masculine environment he was raised in, and I couldn't really fault him for it.

I could still get angry, though.

He must not have sensed the shift in my mood, and if he did, then he'd decided it was best not to acknowledge it. We went into the bar in silence, walking over to a couple of stools tucked in the corner. The place was nice, with exposed brick walls and twinkling rainbow-colored lights around the center of the room, where the bartenders simultaneously worked their smiles and their muscles. I sat with a view looking out to the street, where a younger couple stood and passed a cigarette between them.

Eric grabbed us drinks and came back, setting my Moscow mule down on the table.

"Alright, so since we're on a one-drink timer, maybe we should kick things off," he said, taking a (small) sip of his vodka soda.

"Okay, so you already know about Archie being a hot mess and coming back into the family recently, but you don't know about the blowup he had with my mom. It was bad enough to the point where she threatened to erase his name from the will."

"Shit, so she even brought up her own will?"

"Oh yeah. We were all there. It was during his wedding."

That made Eric's jaw crack. "What was the fight over?"

"Our older sister. Kendall. She and Archie went through a lot of the same things, except Kendall had a much harder time finding her way out of it. Maybe some of it had to do with Archie being my mom's clear favorite, or maybe Kendall just had to hit that rock bottom to be able to bounce back up. Not that she's really bounced back up yet." Loud pop music underscored my words, backed up by the dancers on the television screens hung up above us. "My brother invited Kendall to the wedding without telling my mom. This was like a week after Kendall nearly set my mom's house on fire when she blacked out on shots of tequila for breakfast and knocked over a candle. My mom threatened to walk out of the wedding, but eventually, we were able to talk some sense into her. My dad, William, was wasted before all of this even went down so he wasn't much help."

"Will Kendall be at the family retreat?"

"Mhmm," I said with the straw in my mouth, taking a similarly small sip. If it really was only going to be one drink tonight, then I might as well make it last.

"Did she and your mom ever make up?"

"I'm not entirely sure. I know they were on speaking terms, but I don't know if an official apology was ever said or accepted."

Which sounds kind of familiar, actually.

"And what's your sister's situation like now?" Eric asked.

"Better, but still not great. Definitely not as turned around as Archie. She still couch-surfs from time to time and can't hold down any steady job. She doesn't seem to have any passions, either, but she does say she's sober, so that's at least one good thing going for her right now." I suddenly felt my stomach twist as I looked at Eric's thoughtful gaze. "I mean, you don't think... I don't think Kendall would ever do anything to our mom."

"I know, but I have to look at every possible angle. And there could have been someone hired to do the job. We don't know everything yet."

The twist in my stomach grew tighter. I swallowed a deep breath but felt it get stuck somewhere in my throat, my body reacting to Eric's suggestion with a flood of anxiety.

"God, this is so fucked." I put my head in my hands and let out the breath that had lodged itself in my throat. "I hate this, so fucking much."

"Let's not get ahead of ourselves," Eric said, reaching over and putting a reassuring hand around my wrist. I looked up, finding a warmth and care that I hadn't felt in —well, not since Eric and I were together.

He let go of my wrist, head cocked. "Whatever happens, we have to put it into perspective that it's for your mom. The truth is for her; we just have to find it. And we will."

"But what if the truth is worse than the lie?"

"Sometimes it is, but we'll tackle that monster when

it rears its head. Not before then. Plus, you've got me now." He smirked, his lips shining under the slightly blue lights of the bar. "Bubba. Bubby? What should be our pet names for each other? Junebug. That's yours for sure."

I rolled my eyes and chuckled. "Fine. My birthday is in June anyway. And I'll call you... Teddy. Cuz you're a bear of a man."

Eric's eyebrows drew up. "Huh, just like old times."

"Yup," I said, remembering the days I first started calling him Teddy as a joke, not knowing that Theodore happened to be Eric's middle name. That was back when we were young, dumb, and full of com—*raderie* for each other.

He smiled and nodded. "That works," he said and sat back in his chair, my eyes falling to those plush lips of his.

We stayed at the bar past our one-drink limit, going for three more before I called it a night. Once I started seeing double of Eric (and feeling doubly attracted to him), I realized it was best we went our separate ways. He told me about another book club meeting they were having tomorrow, which sounded like a good time, as well as a neutral space to hang out with him, so I promised him I'd be there.

As we were each waiting for our Ubers, there was a quiet moment between us that felt as though it was going to lead to a kiss. Eric was just telling me how he'd had such a great time today, and he was inching closer and his hand was moving for mine, and my heart started to pound a little harder and— *Honk.*

My ride had pulled up on the other side of the street

and honked to let me know he'd arrived. Eric put his hands in his pocket and said bye, leaving me wondering what would have happened if Jean in his red Toyota had gotten stuck in traffic for a couple of minutes longer on his way to pick me up. Would I have kissed him back?

Damn it, I thought to myself as I got into the car. *We've really got to set up some boundaries. And quick.*

11

ERIC RUIZ

I WAS one of the first to arrive at Tia and Jess's new house. It was a two-story home tucked into a nice Atlanta suburb with a manicured lawn and a couple of hanging potters holding trailing vines on the porch. They had just repainted it so that it was a clean white with a dark blue door, coordinating with the navy cushion on the rocking chair. A couple of neighborhood kids rode their bikes down the street, chasing after each other and laughing at the silly jabs they'd throw to one another.

It was all a huge change from their last neighborhood, which was constantly seeing police activity, red and blue lights occasionally flashing through the closed blinds of their living room window. We'd hear some crazy shit when we were over at their place when the windows were open. Yelling, screeching, sirens, crying. But it had always been a temporary home for them, having to adjust after taking on some big medical debt from Jess's scary (but thankfully brief) fight with breast cancer. It was a fucked-up place to be where medical expenses outweighed things like rent and a down payment for a new house, but the two of them had stuck with each other and fought through it.

Now they had the house of their dreams, with a yard and a pool and a separate room for a baby down the line. It was all they'd ever wanted, and it made me so damn happy to see.

"Hello, new homeowners," I said to a smiling Tia as she opened the door.

Her face dropped. "What did you just call me?" We both cracked up in laughter as I took her in a hug, handing her the bottle of champagne I'd gotten in cele-bration.

"Veuve? Oh, you know that's my favorite. You didn't have to," she said, "but I'm glad you did." She threw her braids over her shoulder and chuckled before leading me inside.

Jess came down the stairs, her bracelets jingling with every bouncing step she took, a wide smile plastered on her dewy, freshly showered face. I could still smell the coconut shampoo she used when she pulled me in for a hug.

"Do I get a tour?" I asked, looking around at the expertly furnished living room. Tia was the interior designer of the pair, while Jess focused more on cheering her on. A bright red leather couch popped against the white carpet, drawing the eye before the large Pollock-inspired paintings took your attention. There were multiple vases holding a cluster of different-colored flowers and orchids, adding a touch of life that made the entire space come together.

The television was on, set to the local news. A reporter stood outside of the police department, the lower third reading: Midnight Chemist strikes again. Atlanta's gay community on high alert.

"Damn, another one?" I shook my head, a sinking feeling settling in my chest and ruining this otherwise delightful moment. "When are they going to find this person?"

"Hopefully soon," Tia said before turning the television off.

"I was at Blake's yesterday, and it was practically a ghost town compared to how it usually is. People don't even want to go out and hang with friends right now."

"It's so fucked-up," Jess said, a hand on the back of her neck. She wore a black T-shirt with the sleeves cut off and a plunging neckline, Lady Gaga rocking out on her chest.

"Come, come," Tia said with a hand on my shoulder. "Let's give you that tour."

The rest of their house was just as well designed and homey as the living room. Tia's home office was probably my favorite room, all exposed wood and bold colors with a porthole window that looked out to their tree-lined yard. There was a built-in bookshelf that was filled from floor to ceiling with books, their spines facing out and color coordinated so that it looked like a rainbow was dripping down the wall. The wall opposite that was covered in dreamy and surreal landscape paintings done by Jess, who was a master when it came to watercolors.

Just as we were wrapping the tour, a knock on the door signaled the arrival of another book club member. Tia went to open the door. I expected Yvette, who was normally punctual, but was surprised instead to see a smiling Colton standing there, holding a round metallic tin.

"Hi there, you must be Colton. I'm Tia."

After hugs and introductions were exchanged, Colton stepped inside and handed the tin over to Tia. "I heard you guys just moved in here; Eric was telling me yesterday about it. I baked you some home-warming brownies. They're cut in the shape of a little house."

Tia and Jess both awwed at the same time.

I didn't know Colton liked to bake. That had never come up when we were together. Was it something new he liked to do? What else about him had changed since our time together? I didn't like to think of him as a completely new person, but six years was a lot of space for someone to change, to evolve.

"You really didn't have to," Tia said.

"But she's glad you did," I said with a wink.

It didn't take long for the rest of the crew to show up. Noah and Jake were all giggly after having gone on a date night to a drag dinner that was set up as a murder-mystery event, while Yvette was happy because there appeared to be a new guy in her life. Overall, everyone in my little family of friends was doing good, and that was all I could ever really ask for. We'd been through some serious shit lately, so seeing us all thriving and together, reading books and talking shit, made my heart happy.

Something else that made me happy? Seeing Colton mixed into the group of smiling faces. We all sat in a loose circle in the living room, Colton perched with his legs crossed underneath him on a bench, both hands around his ankles, and the most innocent fucking grin on his face. He wore a bright blue shirt that made his eyes glow like they were royal jewels on display at some heavily guarded museum. In his lap was a copy of the book we were reading, *A Family Affair* written in bold text across the image of a suburban house, the shadow behind it depicting two people that could either have been making love or trying to murder each other.

It was a good book that started off with a bang: the discovery of a dead body during what was supposed to be a family reunion, except the identity of the body isn't revealed, and the next chapter goes back in time to when the party first started.

"I don't know," Tia said, batting at Noah's suggestion that the dead body was going to be someone from the family. "I think it makes more sense for the family to have murdered someone. They're a big Italian family who stick together through thick and thin. We see that in the third chapter when Enzo represents his own brother in court and gets him off free of charge from a drunken hit-and-run. *After* Enzo possibly interfered with the evidence. This family seems to want to cover each other's backs no matter the cost."

"I agree," Colton said, setting one foot down on the

ground and looking around at the group. His leg bounced, drawing my attention to the way his shorts climbed up his thigh, giving me a good glance of thick muscle dusted in light blond hair. "Plus, there's that moment in the beginning where the grandmother turns to everyone and says, 'Well, what the hell are we going to do about this now?' It gives me the vibe that they're all in on it. If the body was one of their own, I think she would have been much more freaked-out."

"Except the grandmother hates Emilio, the outcast brother, who isn't seen in the intro." It was my turn to point out something I noticed. "We see him a couple chapters later being an absolute mess. Even Enzo, who put himself and his career on the line for him, says he's nearly had enough of his little brother."

"So maybe the dead body is Emilio?" Yvette asked. "But who would have killed him?"

"Should we ask the 8-ball?" Tia leaned forward and grabbed the bedazzled pink 8-ball that sat on the coffee table. This was her game for the night. Whenever someone had a question, we'd ask the 8-ball what it thought. Except each answer had a certain number of drinks attached to it, so asking a question could end up getting you blasted.

She handed the 8-ball to Yvette, who shook it after asking her question again and read the answer out loud. "Keep on searching. And drinking. Take three chugs." Yvette set the ball down on the table and grabbed her cup of vodka cranberry. "Great, I got nothing."

"Except a buzz," Tristan pointed out cheerily.

"I want to ask it something," Jake said, moving his arm from off Noah's shoulders and grabbing the ball. "Was it Emilio who killed someone?"

That got a nod from me. "Maybe that's why he wasn't there in the beginning, because he took off."

"The ball says... It's a possibility, but taking a drink is a certainty." He lifted his glass of champagne and cheered, drinking along with Noah, who grabbed his glass in solidarity. I noticed that they often mirrored one another, whether they realized it or not, even in how they sat, with their legs crossed at the ankles and their bodies leaning toward one another. Even in their body language, the two proved that they were a perfect match.

It was nice to see, but it did make me wonder if I'd ever feel that same connection with someone else.

"Damn, this family is a mess," Tristan said.

Colton gave a huff and leaned back on his seat, stretching his arms over his head. "Sounds like my family."

"It can't be all that bad," Yvette said.

"Eric and I are leaving in a couple of days to go investigate them for the murder of my mother, who left an inheritance that none of us have yet to even see."

Yvette pursed her lips. "Oh. Oh shit, yeah, okay."

Colton laughed, which cracked any ice that may have formed. "But that's what a family is, huh? A messy group of people who love and hate each other through all the different bullshit phases of life."

"You know," Tristan said, setting his book aside and leaning forward, "this little family right here was pretty effective in solving Noah's stalker case last year. Would you maybe consider using the rest of tonight to brainstorm some possibilities? Maybe we can help you guys see something new with what you already have."

Colton's eyebrows rose. He looked around the group, his sapphire-blue orbs seeming to suck me in like a pair of black holes, their gravitational pull impossible to resist. Did Tristan just cross a line? Was Colton ready to open up to a group of people he'd just met? Sure, I was comfortable around the crew, but that was because we were all family at this point. Colton was brand-new, and it wasn't like his situation was an easy one to talk about.

I decided to cut in. We could discuss this some other time. "Maybe we—"

"Yeah, I actually think that's a great idea," Colton said, his big lips curling into a smile.

I should have asked the 8-ball how it saw the night ending. Maybe then I would have called it a night; maybe it would have given me a warning.

Instead, I went on with the night blind to the train that was barreling its way down the tracks in my direction.

12

COLTON COOPER

ERIC WASN'T LYING when he told me that his book club read good books and drank lots of drinks. I was tipsy nearly five minutes into the meeting and totally drunk by the end of it. It was such a great time. And I had been shocked—even in my drunken state—when they suggested setting the book down and focusing on my issue instead. I was going to tell them not to worry about it—I didn't want to bother any of them with my drama— but I changed my mind and instead decided to welcome their help.

The more, the merrier. Maybe one of the book club crew could spot something that Eric or I had missed. Plus, they seemed more than eager to help.

"Maybe your mom had some enemies you don't know about?" Tristan suggested as I wrapped up the summary of what happened.

"Maybe," I said, nodding. "But I doubt it. Everyone loved my mom. She was one of the few rich people that didn't step on everyone's head on her way up the ladder. Always taught us to lead with grace and kindness, so I don't think someone did this because they didn't like her."

"Fair enough," Tristan said.

Tia leaned forward, grabbing her drink and speaking around her straw. "Yeah, it sounds like there's more to this."

"And no one knows what was in the will yet?" Jake asked.

"Nope, just the lawyer."

"Will the lawyer be at the villa?" Eric asked.

My eyes jumped to him. He sat across from me on the love seat with a fluffy red blanket thrown over his lap. The overhead lighting in Tia's living room wasn't really doing anyone any favors, but Eric still looked damn good, the alcohol coursing through my veins making me take even more notice of his good looks than usual.

"She will be," I said, trying to peel my eyes off Eric but finding it difficult to break the spell, even when Yvette asked me a question.

"Huh? Sorry, my head's all over the place," I asked her, managing to break eye contact with Eric before he melted me into the bench I was sitting on.

"Oh, I totally get it. I was just saying that maybe the answer isn't money. Maybe it's love? Or, well, the opposite of love. Was your mom involved with anyone?"

That was a good point and one I unfortunately didn't have much information about. "My mom was really hush-hush with whoever she was dating. She still got along with my dad, but they split up when I was in the fourth grade."

"Was it amicable?" Eric asked. I could tell he was slipping on his detective hat. He leaned forward, his amber-brown eyes taking on a certain intensity to them that made me glued to the bench.

"It was, from what I can remember. Of course, me and my siblings got the sugarcoated version of things. So I guess you'd have to ask him for the full story." I licked my lips, my mouth feeling dry all of a sudden. It wasn't like we were gathered around talking about silly hookup stories or twisty book chapters. We were discussing the murder of my mother with a group of people that had just met me and yet still welcomed me with wide-open arms. It made my chest tighten with emotion.

Growing up, I was always a little bit of a loner. I had a hard time making friends at school. I was shy and reserved and quickly became a target for the bullies once puberty came around and my voice was cracking as much as my wrists were. At some point in high school, one of those ritzy private schools where the kids sometimes had more money than the professors themselves, I ended up accepting it and just came out, taking away some of the sting from the bullies' slurs by saying, "Yeah and?" So what if you yell about me sucking dick as we're switching classes. I shrugged and kept walking, which really pissed off some of the more aggressive bullies. One of them—James St. James, a bully name if I'd ever heard one—yanked me by my book bag and started to fight me with how pissed off he got. Thankfully, there was a teacher nearby that intervened before it got serious, which it easily could have judging by the bloodlust in the guy's eyes.

That's when I got into the gym. I knew I had to be able to protect myself. So I got a personal trainer and went balls to the wall, working out two times a day and keeping track of everything I ate. Turned out I loved it. There was a meditative aspect to working out for me, so I capitalized on that. I used my time at the gym to work through my shit, solve whatever problems I had on my plate at the time.

But still, I was always missing something, and now I realized what that was: a close friend group. One that felt like family. I thought I'd find some of that when I joined the police academy, being encouraged to join by my grandfather, who was a cop all his life. It took a little convincing, but it was during a point in my life when I'd never felt more lost. I wanted to help people, and I wanted to have a job that didn't keep me locked up in an office. The last thing I wanted to do was ride off my mother's coattails, and so I felt like it was one of my only options for having a solid and self-sustaining future.

But instead of brotherly camaraderie, I was confronted with the same brutish personalities that had bullied me when I was younger. The only person I got along with before I dropped out was Eric, and the reasons for that were obvious to me... maybe not so much to him.

"I'll see if I have a chat with your dad," Eric said, pulling me back to the present, even though he'd been right there with me in the past.

"I can't believe you guys are going to be in the South of France in a couple of days," Noah said. He was wearing a black pair of Ray-Bans that he adjusted to sit higher up on his nose.

"Me neither," Eric said with a laugh.

"Are we still having book club night?" Tristan asked, looking around like an excited puppy. "We can Zoom it."

"Yeah, let's do it," I said, clapping my thighs. "I'm really loving this. Thank you, guys, for having me."

"Are you kidding?" Yvette said, getting up and grabbing the empty bottle of wine. "The more, the merrier with us. I love seeing our gay little family keep getting bigger and bigger."

"Speaking of, I invited my neighbor Steven to join. He's new to Atlanta, too." Eric looked down at his phone. "He said he couldn't make it, though."

"Alright, well, hold on," Tia said, hands in the air. "I'm all for growing our club, too, but we're going to need an auditorium for our meetings at this rate."

Jess laughed, cuddling into her wife's side. "We can have an overspill area in our dining room."

Jake reached up to the ceiling for a stretch, covering a yawn at the last minute. I glanced at the clock on the wall, surprised to see how late it had gotten. Tia clapped her hands, likely sensing the exhaustion that was slowly sinking into the room. "Alright, I think we can probably wrap it up there tonight. Next meeting is at Tristan's, but we'll Zoom with our French cuties so they don't have to miss it." She leaned forward and grabbed the bedazzled

8-ball. "Mrs. All-Seeing 8-Ball, do you think Eric and Colton are going to have a good time together in France?"

She gave it a shake. Why the hell was I getting so anxious all of a sudden? As if I'd take anything the ball was about to say seriously.

"Absolutely. Now take a shot."

Oh, thank God.

She set the ball back down on the coffee table and grabbed her water bottle. "I'm taking a shot of Dasani because I have to work early tomorrow, thank you very much." She raised the bottle and gave a cheers before taking a swig.

The group stood up and helped clean a bit before we started to filter toward the door, saying our goodbyes and our thanks to the girls for hosting us. Somehow, Eric and I ended up together on their porch, the rest of the group having already left. My Uber was already waiting for me. I looked out at the quiet night and suddenly realizing I wasn't exactly ready for it to end. Not just yet.

"Do you want to come over?" I asked Eric as we started down the steps toward the street. "We can go over our boundaries and stuff—you know, for the fake relationship we're going to have to pull off."

Eric didn't take much time at all to think over my offer. He smiled and said, "Sure, sounds like a plan," as he hopped into the backseat of the Uber with me.

Boundaries. That's what tonight is about. I've got to remember that.

13

ERIC RUIZ

IT TOOK me a second to really believe the fact that I was currently sitting on Colton's couch, drinking a glass of wine and talking about the time the two of us had spent a weekend in a cabin up in Blue Ridge. It was a week before our big fight, and it had been one of the best staycations of my life. We'd spent it playing video games —naked, of course—using the joysticks on the controllers, along with the ones between our legs. We had sex on practically every surface of that one-bedroom secluded cabin, surrounded by trees and nature and fresh air. It was the first time the two of us were truly alone, without the chance of being interrupted by someone, and that made the weekend feel all the more special.

It had also scared me. Made me realize that I had fallen hard for Colton, beyond just the physical aspect—I had really fallen for the person Colton was. And being deep in the closet at the time made that realization feel like I'd been stabbed in the chest. I knew what I had to do.

I cut it all off. A week later, a week after the best damn days of my life with the best damn man in my life.

"You kicked my ass in Super Smash that weekend," Colton said. "You and your Mewtwo main."

"Yeah, but then I kissed your ass afterwards to make it all better." I shot Colton a smirk and took a sip of the wine, my muscles slowly turning to liquid as the alcohol did its job. My inhibitions were lowered, which made these flirty comments fly out without any second thought behind them.

Colton shook his head and looked away. I noticed a red flush creep up the side of his neck, but he shifted on the chair so that he looked directly at me. Had I gone too far?

"Whatever, man," Colton said, his lips curling into a smirk. "I bet I could beat you now."

"Do you have it?"

"Mhmm," he said, standing up and going over to the large entertainment console underneath the television, which had a changing screensaver that made it appear as if it were a hanging piece of art. Currently, a dreamy midnight scene of a lake and a couple set inside a modern black frame took up the entire screen. Colton grabbed two controllers and pressed the power button on the gaming console, the screen switching on and the art being replaced by a simple and clean white interface.

"Damn, I haven't played this in years," I said as

Colton handed me the controller and took a seat on the couch next to me.

"Good, so then I really do have a chance."

"I wouldn't go that far," I teased. "I've still got muscle memory."

Turned out I actually *didn't* have any muscle memory. Not when it came to video games, at least. Colton proved his skills by launching me off the screen about five times in under two minutes, earning him a win. He jumped up from the couch and did a little victory dance, which had him wiggling his butt in a way that had me hypnotized.

"Rematch?" I asked when Colton calmed down. He fell back on the couch and grabbed his controller. There was less space between us this time, with his knee nearly touching mine.

Just like old times...

Except, if it really *were* just like old times, Colton and I would be pants-less with his leg thrown over mine, our video games breaks consisting of us playing with each other.

We went a couple more rounds, all of them going to Colton until the very last one, when the skills started coming back to me and I was able to claim a victory.

Colton set the controller down on the side table next to the couch. He stretched out, taking off his socks by rubbing them on the floor. He grabbed them and bundled them together, setting them to the side.

Something about Colton being barefoot made the room get about ten degrees hotter. I wasn't totally obsessed with feet, but Colton's feet were about to change that.

...Maybe because I could vividly recall how it felt when I was kissing them as I slowly fucked him, his legs up on my chest and his eyes rolling back in his head and his... fuck.

I was hard. Rock hard. I grabbed a yellow pillow and placed it on my lap, trying to cover the obvious bulge Colton was giving me.

And we're supposed to talk about boundaries tonight. Great.

As if on cue, Colton stood up, looking down at me with his head cocked. "Alright, want another glass of wine before we get started? I think I'm going to make myself some popcorn."

"Go for it," I said.

"Come with me to the kitchen. I can show you what I did to it."

"I, uhm, have to check some emails," I said as my cock gave a rogue twitch underneath the pillow.

"Seriously? At ten in the evening?"

I grabbed my phone and tried to ignore the throbbing between my legs. "Yeah, I had to transfer all my cases over to a new PI before leaving. There's a place I've worked with in the past, Stonewall Investigations, and they're opening up a new spot here, so they were just seeing if they could take on my caseload."

While I picture dropping my load all over your face.

Fuck, I was horny. I'd have to deal with this on my own later.

"Gotcha," Colton said, walking over to his kitchen. There was a long cutout in the wall that separated the two rooms so he could still see me, which meant I was keeping this pillow on my lap until my body decided it was time to calm the hell down.

The beeps of the microwave sounded off in the kitchen, followed by the familiar sound of popping popcorn. I glanced up, seeing Colton leaning against the kitchen counter, looking at the microwave so that his back was turned toward me. I took a second to adjust my slowly softening dick and went back to checking emails, relieved to see one that confirmed my cases were being taken up by Stonewall.

"So?" Colton asked as he returned with a bowl of popcorn and another beer. "Are they taking them?"

"Yes, thankfully." I sniffed the air and looked over at the bowl. "People never change, do they?"

Colton rolled his eyes and sat down. "Are you talking about my slightly burnt popcorn?"

"Yes, I think you might be the only human being with a functioning set of taste buds that enjoys eating burnt popcorn."

"*Slightly* burnt popcorn. And so what? It's like asking for your steak well-done, except this is easier to cook."

I laughed at the fact that Colton considered himself a chef after microwaving a bag of popcorn for ten seconds longer than recommended.

"You sure you don't want some?" he asked, tipping the bowl in my direction.

"I'm good. Thanks, though."

He shrugged and grabbed a handful, popping them in his mouth and speaking before he even finished swallowing. "Boundaries. We gotta talk about them. I think it's fine if we do the boyfriend stuff in front of other people, like hold hands and kiss on the cheek or whatever, but only when it's in front of people. It needs to feel like an act."

I sucked in a breath. "Fair enough," I said, suddenly wondering how the hell I was going to get through the next two weeks without fantasizing about Colton every second of every day.

"And we have to limit ourselves—only two kisses a day. So choose wisely."

"Two kisses each?" I tossed out, even though a hundred sounded like a much more reasonable number to me.

"Sure, two kisses each." Colton tipped his head back, looking up at the ceiling and exposing his neck in a way that made my mouth water. "Sleeping situation?"

"I think being in the same room makes the most sense." Colton nodded as I continued. "But if there's a couch or a roll-out bed, I'll take that, and you just get the regular bed."

Even though sleeping next to Colton would be a wet dream come true, I wanted to work overtime to make him comfortable. I was there for a job, and it was likely one of the most important jobs of my career; the last thing I wanted to do was cross any lines and make Colton regret hiring me. I didn't want to disappoint him... or hurt him. Not again.

"We'll figure out the sleeping arrangement when we get there. If we've got to share a bed and put pillows between us, then fine." Colton grabbed another handful of slightly singed popcorn. "I think we'll be good."

"I'm sure we'll be good. Everything's going to work out. I'll be able to scope out your family in a way a regular detective wouldn't be able to, basically going undercover so that I can figure out what happened to your mom. Asking housekeeping for a couple of extra pillows is one of the last things I'm worried about." I glanced at the clock, surprised to see it was already midnight. The day had flown right on by.

"What *are* you worried about?" Colton's question caught me a little off guard. I didn't want him to think there was something that concerned me, even though there were quite a few things that made me nervous.

Failing to find out what happened to Amelia.

Getting discovered as a fraud by your family.

Developing feelings for you all over again.

Exposing myself to major heartbreak. All over again.

"Nothing much," I said, drinking a big chug of white wine. I didn't do fears—at least, I didn't like talking about them. Same with emotions. I kept things off to the side, slowly processing them on my own. Sharing my anxieties with Colton wasn't going to help the situation in any way.

"Really? Nothing? Because I can name about six things off the top of my head that have me up at night."

I reached a hand out, squeezing his shoulder. It was meant as a friendly gesture, but my hand lingered for a moment longer than normal, my fingers slowly grazing off the slope of his muscular frame. "Whatever comes up won't be anything I can't handle. Don't worry, you're in good hands with me."

Colton sighed. He picked up his wineglass and gave it a swirl, the legs of the wine sticking to the sides of the glass as he watched it settle. "This isn't a mistake, right?"

"Absolutely not."

"I'm not overreacting, right?"

I shook my head, moved a little closer to Colton on the couch. "I think you have plenty of reason to be suspicious."

"But of who? My sister, my brother? My *dad*? I hate suspecting any of them."

Colton rubbed his face. I could see the stress rising through him, envisioning steam whistling out of his ears and nose. I hated to see him this riled up. Colton had too bright of a smile to be replaced by the frown he currently wore.

"Maybe it was none of them. But maybe one of them happens to know something that points me in the right direction. Some kind of business connection that wasn't widely shared or a romantic connection that went sour. It could be anything, so let's not get too ahead of ourselves here." I reached out for him again, this time leaving my hand on his shoulder. "Okay?"

He looked into my eyes, and that smile of his returned, slowly but surely. "How do you do that?"

"What?"

"Make things always feel like they're going to turn

out alright. Even when we were tog—when we were younger, you always knew how to make me feel better about something." His blue eyes glittered under the warm light shining from the floor lamp.

"I think it's because I always look for the positive in things. My mom's a big optimist. I got it from her." I squeezed his shoulder and let go, but I dropped my hand on his thigh instead. He looked down, smile still on his face.

"Should we discuss boundaries with touching?" he asked, eyebrow arched, dimple on his cheek looking like a crater because of his smile.

"I think we should touch, often, just to keep up appearances."

He licked his lips, hand falling on mine. His warmth encased me as his fingers closed around me. Was he about to push me away? I might have crossed a line. I had to remember that Colton was on a different wavelength than me. He wasn't ready to open himself up to a real relationship yet, and I had to respect that...

He moved my hand up, higher on his thigh. His eyes glittered with something else now, his lids narrowing, his lips shining in the light. "And when should these boundaries and rules kick in?"

"Tomorrow?" I said, moving closer, my eyes locked on Colton's lips.

"Tomorrow it is."

And before I knew it, we were kissing. Hard and wet and hungry.

It felt like being caught in a landslide. The primal

power of the earth itself was pushing us together, making our bodies collide in a way that echoed a collision of stars, creating an entire universe of possibility and heat and want.

I encased his head in my hands as we kissed. My lungs filled with his breath, my tongue gliding over his in a way that felt familiar and new and oh so fucking right. He tasted like heaven, my body flooding with an intoxicating mix of endorphins and adrenaline. This wasn't supposed to be happening—we were supposed to be keeping things off-limits. We needed to keep things clean between us.

But I didn't want this kiss to ever stop. We could deal with the consequences of it later. For now, for tonight, for this midnight, all I wanted to do was sink into Colton, to lose myself like I'd done so many midnights before, boundaries and rules and history be fucking damned.

14

COLTON COOPER

THIS WAS GOING against everything I'd mentally prepared for, and yet it felt like it was the only thing I'd ever really wanted. My defenses instantly crumbled when Eric's lips reunited with mine. Sparks flew through the air as my breath hitched in my lungs. He had stolen it directly from me, leaving me gasping, yearning for more. Kissing him back might not have been the best idea considering my heartbroken state, but I couldn't help it.

How could I ever turn Eric down? No, that was an impossible task.

So I kissed him back hard, sighing into his mouth as his hands grabbed my head. He steered our kiss, nipping at my top lip before probing me with his tongue, his taste exploding all across my mouth. Another moan escaped me, swallowed instantly by a scorching hot Eric, his hands moving down my back, sliding under my shirt.

"Is this okay?" he asked with big brown puppy-dog eyes.

Damn him. Damn him for caring, for even asking. It only made me want him more.

"It's more than okay," I said in between breaths as I smashed my lips back against his. It was my turn to take over some of the control. I moved my leg over his, climbing onto his lip. I was pleasantly surprised to feel what felt like an iron rod being smuggled inside Eric's pants.

I ground my ass down on him, kissing him with a smile as he throbbed underneath me. Any reservations I had about tonight caught flames in that moment, burning to a crisp and leaving behind only ash. Being with Eric, alone in my living room, his hard cock pressing up against me, it threw me right back to when we were together, when the world felt so perfect and right. I'd been on top of the world whenever I was on top of Eric, and tonight was no different.

Eric broke from the kiss and moved down to my neck, sucking on the spot that always drove me absolutely feral. I dropped my head back and moaned, louder than intended, as heat rose up my chest, climbing up my neck, focusing on the spot where Eric grazed his teeth and licked his tongue. My thoughts quickly scrambled, as if my brain had been dropped onto a sizzling frying pan.

"Take this off," I said, tugging at his shirt before I pulled mine over my head. I leaned back and watched as Eric took off his shirt, revealing the sexiest chest and stomach I'd ever fucking seen. He was covered in a soft dusting of dark hair, concentrated mostly around the center of his chest and trailing down over his belly, leading down to a tuft of hair sticking out from the waistband of his low jeans.

I rubbed him up and down, leaning in and kissing his ear, feeling his heartbeat just underneath my fingertips as I grazed over his pebbled nipples. I squeezed, earning a moan that made my cock ache to be sucked.

I palmed myself as I moved downward, taking a nipple in my mouth and swirling my tongue as I held it between my teeth. Eric rubbed my back, the sounds coming from him only growing louder. He thrust up, rubbing himself on me. The AC was on in my house, but it felt like it was just about to hit a hundred degrees in here.

More. I needed more. I got down to the floor, falling to my knees as I opened Eric's legs. We were really doing this. After nearly seven years apart, I was back to being in my favorite spot in the entire fucking universe. Right here, between Eric's big legs, my head fitting perfectly between his thighs.

I unzipped his pants and had him naked in seconds, his cock springing free, head glistening. I leaned back to admire him for a moment, licking my lips as I watched him throb. His balls hung heavy, shifting ever so slightly, adjusting to the air, hypnotizing me. I leaned forward and took one in my mouth.

"Fuuucking hell, Colton. That's it. Swallow the other one. Yeah, you like my balls, huh?"

I nodded and said, "Yes, sir," which came out muffled from the amount of nut I had in my mouth. His hands came to rest on the top of my head, guiding me up his shaft. I licked his cock, taking him in my mouth. His salty precum coated my tongue as I licked his slit, swallowing everything he had to give me.

"Take it. That's it, baby. Swallow that cock. Make it disappear down your throat, just like that."

Eric's words were lighting a fire inside of me. My hole twitched, my body craving to be one with this man. I took more of him into my mouth, earning an animalistic grunt as he pulled on my hair and stuffed himself further down my throat. With a free hand, wet from my own saliva, I reached back and slipped it under my underwear, finding my hole and rubbing, teasing, slipping inside without much resistance at all. I moaned with a mouthful of cock as I fingered myself, looking up into Eric's eyes as I did it.

"Play with that sexy ass, baby. Fuck, do you realize how hot you are?"

I just looked up at him, pulling off his cock for a breath as my finger slipped deeper inside, my cock leaking a puddle of precum into my Calvins.

Things were quickly escalating. Lust clouded every single thought I had, painting the room in shades of reds and pinks. Heat consumed me as Eric's taste flooded over me.

More. More. *More.*

I stopped blowing him, stroking him instead, enjoying how thick he felt in my grip.

Having him in my hands, his velvet-hot heat coursing through my palms, it wasn't enough. I needed more. I *knew* I needed more, even though it might have been the final nail in my coffin.

I got up, took off my precum-stained underwear, and tossed it in the pile of discarded clothes, looking down at a rock-hard Eric. He ate me up with his eyes, raking over me from my feet up to my head, lingering on my cock.

I climbed back onto his lap, bracing both legs on either side of him as I lined his cock up with my hole.

"I need you to fuck me, Eric. The way you used to. Just for tonight."

I looked down into Eric's eyes, seeing a blazing hot fire reflected back up at me.

"You sure?" he asked while pushing his hips up, rubbing the head of his cock against me.

"Yes, Eric, please. I'm sure." I spat in my hand and reached back, getting him slick with a couple of tight strokes. "Have you been tested?"

"Yes, and it's all negative. I'm on PrEP, too."

"Same here."

I trusted Eric. With anyone else, I would have pressed pause and gone for a condom, but there was an ingrained sense of honesty and trust between us that made it easy to let all my worries slip off into the night.

I looked up at the clock. Five minutes to midnight. Soon, Eric and I would be flying across the globe to pretend like we were boyfriends so that my family could open up to him. In five minutes, our boundaries and rules would be officially in place, making something like this totally off-limits.

Five minutes.

I had a feeling I only needed half that time. My cock leaked onto Eric's dark treasure trail as I sank back, gasping as the head of his cock opened me up. I controlled my breathing and relaxed my body, focusing on the intense hunger that radiated out from my core. Telling me to be one with Eric, to take him inside me, and to ride him until the stars fell from the sky.

"God, Eric, you feel so good inside me."

"Oh shit, Colt. Fuck, I don't think I'm going to last long."

I put a hand on his chest and sank down so that his entire length pushed into me, my swollen prostate rubbing against him. Lightning bolts exploded through the room. I threw my head back and cried out as Eric started to fuck me, finding a rhythm where I was able to bounce down, pushing him in deeper.

Harder. Faster. Oh fuck. Fuck, fuck, *fuck*.

"Keep going," I said, falling forward so that my head nestled into Eric's neck while he plowed into me. His hands dug into my hips as he worked me, giving me exactly what I needed, what I had begged for. "Keep going, Eric. Fuck, you're going to fucking make me come."

"Do it, baby. Spray your load all over my chest."

I sat back up as the wave crested over my body, crashing over me with a primal force. My load covered Eric's entire chest as my body convulsed, squeezing and contracting around Eric. He dropped his head back and growled like a caged lion, plunging himself deep before holding there, filling me with his orgasm.

A residual growl escaped his throat as I slowly pulled off him, come sliding down my thigh. I smiled, my entire being lifted up past the clouds, drifting somewhere past Mars. This broke every single rule we meant to set up, but it was worth it for this floaty, fuzzy feeling.

I got a warm, wet towel from the bathroom and came back to clean Eric up before I cleaned myself up. I came back to the living room with fresh glasses of ice-cold water, which Eric thanked me for, still sitting naked and breathless on my couch.

It was a sight I don't think I'd ever get tired of seeing. "That was... just like old times," Eric said as I sat down.

"Even better," I said, smiling as I rubbed my chest, throwing a casual leg over Eric's. "There's something sexier than ever about your confidence."

"I do feel way more confident now than I ever have."

I nodded, closing my eyes as Eric massaged my calf. "It looks good on you. And feels good in me."

He chuckled and continued to massage me, the room lapsing into a comfortable silence. At one point, his massaging stopped, but his hand didn't leave me. Instead, he started to trace lines with his fingers—no, those weren't lines. They were letters.

I smiled so wide my cheeks started to hurt.

"Kiss me," I said, reading the words he wrote on my skin.

"I was wondering if you still had it," Eric said as I went in for a smoldering kiss, one that carried the memories of all those nights we spent together, when Eric and I would trace invisible words on each other. It was our way of being discreet in public together. If we were ever in a lineup or standing close to each other, we'd get to writing, scrawling invisible words on each other to assure us we were still together. Like high schoolers in a secret relationship, sharing notes as they passed each other in the hallways.

A silence that left too much room for my thoughts to wander. I started to think about our baggage, and how even after Eric rearranged my guts in the best way possible, we still needed to talk about what happened between us. Maybe now wasn't the most opportune time, but all of my filters were annihilated, so any thoughts that entered my brain were liable to slip right on out.

"You know," I said, "we spent a lot of time talking about what's coming up, but I don't think we've spent any time about what happened with us. Our past."

I heard Eric suck in a breath.

"It's hard, I know," I said, sitting up on the couch. My entire body was spent, but my heart started to race again. Eric's chest was still flushed, his tan cheeks getting a little bit of extra color as well. "But we have to talk about it."

"Maybe now's not the best time?" he said, deflecting once again.

"It's never really the *best* time for that sort of thing, is it? We just have to rip it off like a Band-Aid. The sooner we do it, the better."

He took another breath, his gaze drifting to somewhere in the distance, somewhere that wasn't in my living room. It brought me back to the old days, and not in a good way. It reminded me of how he'd always deflect whenever I tried to have a serious conversation with him.

He had seemed incapable of discussing anything having to do with us or his emotions.

Had he changed for the better, or was he even more closed off than before?

"We've started back up on such a great foot, though. Why ruin it?"

Okay, so it was the latter. He didn't even want to broach the topic of our past.

But I did. "I don't think that having an adult conversation about the things you did to hurt me is ruining what we've got going now."

Eric's eyebrows jerked up his forehead as if I'd said something that surprised him. "I—you left that night, cursing me out. And I explained why I felt like we couldn't keep doing what we were doing. I didn't realize—"

"That you completely crushed my heart and made it hard for me to open up to anyone for a pretty long time? Yeah, well, you did." Now I was beginning to feel spicy. I had let this man inside me, sharing one of the most intimate parts of me with him, and I wanted every fucking second of it, every inch of him. But now, annoyance was mixing with frustration, a concoction of emotions that pushed away the residual bliss I was feeling from my orgasm.

All he had to do was say sorry, and for a split second, those were the exact words I expected to hear from him.

"I'm... I'm just really surprised. I thought you understood my reasoning."

My jaw dropped. That was not where I saw this

conversation headed. I felt like I'd been slapped. Was I dumb? Should I have never even invited him over to my house in the first place?

"I understood you were deep in the closet, and yes, that sucks, but that doesn't take away from the pain I experienced, Eric. The pain you caused."

He shook his head, his gaze lowering to the floor, where our underwear still lay in a bundle. I got off the couch and reached down, grabbing his and tossing it onto his chest.

"Here, get dressed and go," I said, already over it. I knew this was a mistake. Just like he had called me all those nights ago, lightning crashing outside with the same intensity as the fracturing inside my chest. "It's already twelve thirty. The rules we talked about are in full effect. We'll get through this trip and go our separate ways when it's over, hopefully with answers about my mom's death. I don't think we should see each other before we get to the villa."

I pulled on my black briefs, the fabric still stained from the precum Eric had made me ooze.

Fucking damn it. Why did he have to be like this? Why did he have to have the emotional maturity of a dusty rock? If only he could apologize, if only he could tell me he was sorry, then maybe I'd consider tossing these boundaries and rules out the window.

But he didn't, and neither did I. He got dressed in silence and walked himself to the door as I poured a glass of water.

"Colton, I'm—"

"Just go, Eric. I'll see you in France."

I closed the door, locked it, and went to my bed, where I got in and under the covers, going to sleep with the scent of Eric still on my lips and the ghost of his pain still on my heart.

15

ERIC RUIZ

AN IMAGINE DRAGONS song played through my headphones as the car drove me through the scenic French countryside, down winding roads that wrapped around large fields of olive groves framed by a couple of rolling hills covered in pine trees. We were staying in a town called Provence, which was only a stone's throw away from the more well-known towns of Nice and Cannes. I had absolutely no time to brush up on my French, but thankfully, the driver spoke enough English to get by, telling me a couple of interesting facts about Provence before we lapsed into silence, and I put my headphones back in.

I had to clear my head. The next couple of weeks were crucial in figuring out what had happened to Amelia, and that meant I had to be at the top of my game. So the drama between Colton and me had to be put on ice. At least for now.

He had arrived a day earlier, telling his family that I'd

had something to wrap up at work. They were under the impression that I was a high-powered attorney working criminal defense cases in New York. I had worked with plenty of attorneys in my career as a PI, so it wasn't that far of a leap from the truth; I just hoped I picked up enough legalese to pull off any surface questions I might be asked.

I was *also* hoping Colton was in better spirits than when I'd last left him. That night had somehow gone from one of the best to one of the worst in a matter of minutes. I'd been ready to go for round two, three, and four. Instead, I was practically pushed out of his home with my underwear on backward and my head in my hands.

Shit sucked. And I wasn't entirely sure what I could have done to remedy it. Did Colton expect me to go back in time and change my choices? I regretted them, there was no doubt about that, but I also couldn't do anything about them. All I could do was prove that I had changed, but it was looking like I wouldn't even get the chance.

I decided to stick to the rules and boundaries we had laid out. No more kissing or touching or fucking. None of that. We were going to play out this fake-boyfriend thing, and I was going to figure out what happened to his mom, and that would be the end of the story. Done. Lights out. Curtains up.

The driver slowed down as he pulled up to a set of curling iron gates flanked by emerald-green hedges that looked trimmed down to the tiniest leaf, making them perfect squares. He buzzed the intercom and spoke something to whoever answered. A loud beep followed as the gates began to swing open.

It started to hit me then. Just yesterday, I had been sitting on my living room couch in Atlanta, going over the details for the case, and now we were pulling up to a sprawling villa tucked into the hills of the South of France, surrounded by fields of lavender. If someone told me this was where I'd find myself after randomly bumping into Colton Cooper in a coffee shop, I would laugh in their face and promptly turn around, hoping they found the help they so clearly needed.

"Here we are, sir," the driver said as it drove around a fountain featuring three angels, the water flowing out of their open hands, their marble wings sculpted to look as if they were in motion at all times. But the fountain only had my attention for a few moments before I looked to the massive villa. With arching doors and windows galore, it looked like something taken directly out of the pages of *Architectural Digest*, all beiges and blacks and whites, with interesting angles that didn't disrupt the flow of the house at all, only enhanced it. I was captivated.

We're staying here? Jesus.

I got out of the car, the driver having already taken my luggage out of the trunk. I thanked him with a generous tip. The gentle scent of the lavender bushes wafted in my direction.

"Merci beaucoup," he said, smiling as he pocketed the money and got back into the black town car.

I expected Colton to come and greet me, but the first person out the door was his sister Jen. She appeared to be sipping on an Aperol spritz, wearing a teal bikini with a white shawl around her hips, her long hair falling down her shoulders in a silky waterfall. I recognized her after studying pictures of the entire family. She was the closest sibling to Colton, who considered her one of his best friends. They had decided to keep her out of the loop in regards to their arrangement since Colton said she always had trouble keeping secrets, but she certainly wasn't high on my suspect list.

"Hey there, you must be Eric. Colton's boyfriend."

"I am," I said, holding out a hand but getting it batted away for a hug instead.

"I'm Jen. Great to finally meet you. I can't believe Colton kept you a secret for this long."

"I know. I can't believe it, either," I said, smiling. "Happy to meet you and to be here. Wow, this is stunning." I spun in a slow circle, taking it all in.

"Isn't it? My mom wanted all that lavender planted. Started with a couple bushes and then turned into an entire field."

It was truly marvelous. Like we had been dropped into the center of a purple ocean, gently swaying in the wind. The rolling hills behind the villa were covered in the bright purple plant, giving the landscape an almost alien quality to it.

Stunning.

"You haven't even seen the inside yet," Jen said. "Come, come. Did you bring a bathing suit? We're all jumping into the heated pool."

"I did," I said, grabbing my suitcase and heaving it up

the three steps and onto the landing, where I rolled it into the foyer, which was as breathtaking as the outside, if not more. It had a vaulted ceiling with exposed beams that ran perpendicular to a dazzling chandelier hung above a sunken seating area that reminded me of the places in my grandmother's house that no one went near, much less sat on, for fear of messing up the expensive furniture.

I could hear the sounds of a party through one of the open archways. Music and laughter and casual conversation. I pulled out my phone and texted Colton a quick "I'm here" in case he wasn't aware.

"Your guys' bedroom is down this hall. It's the one closest to the garden, and it's one of my personal faves." Jen walked ahead of me down a sun-drenched hallway. A door opened on my left, a couple walking out and nearly bumping into me.

"Oh, hey there," the man said. It was Archie with his wife, Wendy, both looking like they were ready to jump in the pool, colorful towels thrown over their shoulders. He was someone I had a close eye on. Off instant impressions, Archie was a smiley guy who closely resembled his little brother: perfectly cut and styled blond hair, bright blue eyes, and a jawline that would make any Superman cosplayer extraordinarily jealous.

Wendy was equally as gorgeous, with a sharp cut to her raven-black hair that made the modelesque angles of her face pop, but her wide smile and warm hazel eyes helped make her less intimidating and more welcoming. She had an arm casually looped around Archie's bare waist, head nearly resting on his shoulder.

"I'm Eric, Col—"

"He's my boyfriend," rang out a cheery (and already drunk) voice from down the hall. I turned to see a dripping wet Colton, towel wrapped around his waist, his perfect six-pack on full display.

Fuckin' hell, how is he so hot?

Colton came straight for me, smile plastered on his face, bare feet padding across the shining marble floor. He opened his arms and took me into a moist hug, kissing me on the lips like any regular boyfriend would do.

Okay. So far, so good.

But damn it, I couldn't deny a not-so-fake spark lighting my chest up like a firework when our lips touched. How the hell was I going to get through this without catching any feelings?

Or worse: what if they'd already been caught?

"Here, I'll grab your suitcase," Colton said, hand wrapping around mine and gently tugging the suitcase from my grip. Archie and Wendy excused themselves, heading down the hall toward where I assumed the pool to be. Jen followed them, saying again how great it was to finally meet me and giving her brother a playful wink and a not-so-discreet thumbs up.

I followed Colton in silence to the end of the hallway, where we turned into our bedroom. There was a four-post bed sitting dead center in the room, with one of the walls covered in a dark green and pink floral wallpaper that easily could have been considered gaudy if it were placed anywhere other than a five-star French villa. I noticed that besides the bed, there were only two other chairs in the room, bordering an arching window, and neither of those chairs looked comfortable enough to sleep in.

Guess we were going to need extra pillows after all.

Colton closed the door, and his smile dropped. He leaned against the wall, arms crossed. "How was your flight?" he asked in the driest tone possible.

Damn. Maybe we weren't even going to need the extra pillows. Colton had formed enough ice between us to easily keep us separated.

16

COLTON COOPER

I WAS STILL PISSED. Couldn't hide it. Seeing Eric again brought back all those emotions I'd been trying to unpack since our night together. I thought I'd gotten over it, but the kiss I'd given him out in the hall made it all come rushing right back.

How were we going to get through the next two weeks of this?

"My flight was fine," Eric said, rolling his suitcase to a corner of the room and looking out the window at the garden, full of purple lavender bushes and bright red roses. He wore a pair of black sweatpants and a gray T-shirt, his hair slightly messy but still perfect somehow, even after nine hours of flying. "How's everything been here?"

I shrugged, prying my eyes off him as he turned around to face me. "They've been fine. A lot of crying the first night. It's the first time we're here without Mom, so that's rough, but I know she'd want us to have a good time. And to figure out what the hell happened to her."

"That's why I'm here," he said, turning his attention to his suitcase. He laid it on the floor and kneeled down, his shirt hitching so that a sliver of tan skin peeked from underneath, sprinkled in a light patch of hair.

I looked back out the window, knowing that my bathing suit and towel would do nothing to hide any unwanted boners. Because even with how annoyed I was at Eric, I could already feel my core tightening at the idea of dropping this towel and getting behind him.

"Is everyone here already?" Eric asked. He pulled out a pair of hot pink swim trunks.

"Grandma Macy and her wife, Luna, should be getting here in time for dinner today, but other than that, everyone is here. Plus, a surprise guest."

"Who's that?" Eric asked.

"Jax, my mom's lawyer. He was supposed to be here to just read the will but surprised us when he showed up holding my sister's hand. Apparently, they're a thing now."

"Which sister? Kendall?"

I nodded, brow arched. "She continues to prove she's the messiest of all. No one had any idea she was going to show up with someone, much less the lawyer."

"Sounds a little familiar," Eric said with a wink. I rolled my eyes but couldn't tamp down my smile.

"Whatever. Change into your swim trunks and meet me in the hallway," I said, moving over to the door as Eric dropped his sweatpants. I wasn't exactly sure he needed the modesty from me, considering he'd been inside me only a couple of days ago, but I gave it to him anyway. If only for my own sanity.

He came out into the hall wearing his bathing suit and a tank top, a silver necklace shining around his neck. How did he manage to look that good after such a long day of traveling?

"Ready?" I asked, already starting down the hall.

"Let's go get wet," Eric said.

I rolled my eyes but couldn't stop the chuckle from escaping. He walked next to me as we traversed the empty hall, following the sounds of splashing and laughter. The house was built in a loose U-shape, with the pool being at the center of the backyard, so it didn't take us long at all to reach it.

Playing a game of water basketball were my brothers Archie and Matthew, while their respective wife and girlfriend provided their support from the side of the pool, where they lounged on half-submerged chairs. The sun beat down on the smooth stone floor that surrounded the large pool, making me hop my way over so that the soles of my feet didn't get singed. Eric followed close behind, taking fewer hops because apparently his feet were made out of fire-resistant material.

"Hey, y'all. This is Eric, my boyfriend. Everyone, say hi," I announced as I got ankle-deep in the water.

Eric waved as the chorus of hellos and welcomes carried through the air. Matthew, the one closest to Eric, stood up and offered a friendly handshake. He was the youngest of the siblings, having only just started college two months ago. He was also likely the most well-adjusted out of all of us. He'd had a long-term girlfriend for a few years now and was set on becoming a doctor, a heart surgeon to be exact. He had the smarts for it, along with the drive; I just worried about how difficult these last couple of months had been on him. I didn't want him getting caught up in any distractions, especially since our mother's death gave him plenty of reason to look for those distractions.

"Wanna jump in the game for me?" Matthew said, handing over the bright blue and white basketball over to Eric. "I've got to go pee."

Eric took the ball and fell forward into the water, splashing me in the process. I wiped my face and waded over to an open lounge chair next to Krystine, Matthew's girlfriend. "Who's winning?" I asked.

"Definitely not Matt," Krystine said. "Hopefully he's got a chance with Eric scoring some points now."

"I wouldn't count on that," I said as Eric took a shot that was quickly blocked by an extremely competitive Archie.

"He's a cutie," Krystine said in a quieter voice, barely louder than the music that played from the Bose speakers. "Good job. You two are, like, the perfect match." She lifted her glass in my direction and gave me a wink before taking a chug through her straw.

"Thanks," I said, as if I'd had some part in making him that good-looking.

As if we're even together in the first place.

That thought stung like a thorn impaled into my side.

I didn't realize how difficult faking this relationship could potentially be. I wasn't counting on people commenting about Eric's looks or how well we fit together. Krystine had barely even seen us interacting, and she was already speaking as if there were wedding bells in the air. At least that meant this relationship wouldn't be a difficult sell to my family, but what the hell did that mean for *us*?

"Where'd you two meet?" she asked as she leaned over, letting one hand make lazy circles in the warm water.

Great. One of the first things we'd prepared for. No big deal. "Online."

Wait... did we say we met online? Crap, I can't remember.

"Oh, nice. I feel like that's just the way to do it lately. Who wants to go and have to put up with small talk at some bar that smells like piss and Natty Light? Might as well go through that BS while I'm at home watching *Below Deck*."

I laughed at that, agreeing wholeheartedly. "Have you been watching this season?"

"Are you kidding me? Does a yachtie piss on a yacht? Yes. The answer is yes." She lay back in the chair and took another sip of her drink. Krystine was the only girl Matt had ever brought home, and I could see why. She had a great sense of humor, always looked good, and— probably most importantly—she was a staunch LGBTQ+ ally, always coming out to Pride parades decked out in rainbows from head to toe. It wasn't always like that with the partners my siblings had brought home. Especially

Kendall, who had a flavor for guys steeped in toxic masculinity. And for someone who was already dealing with some heavy shit, toxic guys who couldn't handle a flirty comment from a drag queen were the *last* thing she needed.

And now she's with Mom's lawyer.

At least I knew this guy had a steady job. I hadn't interacted with him outside of emails, so I couldn't really vouch for his character, but he had worked with my mom for years, so he must have shown some kind of good qualities. I glanced at my watch, wondering when they'd show up.

So far, the family trip was drama-free, without any tempers flaring or egos clashing. But money still hadn't been brought up, and I understood the power money had over people. It could dredge up old arguments and relight long-dead feuds. Archie and Kendall never got along, while Jen had issues with Archie's wife, who had yet to say more than three words to me since we had arrived.

And then there was my dad, William, who was probably out driving around the French countryside. He was a hothead. A good father, but he had a temper that could flare at the smallest of things. It had never been directed at my mother and was always tempered when it was directed at us, but that didn't stop us from seeing him blow up on other people, sometimes for things as tiny as a parking spot.

He had also loved my mom to absolute bits, worshipping not only the ground she walked on but the sky she walked under, too. Everything about her he loved and admired. Their breakup came as a shock to the entire family, but I think it shook my dad more than anything else could have. An alert warning of an incoming nuclear missile could have popped up on his phone and he still would have handled it better than when my mom asked him for a divorce.

But that was years ago now, and he seemed to have dealt with it, finding a space where he and Mom could be friends again.

I chatted with Krystine about *Below Deck* while Eric continued to lose his game of pickup pool basketball. They wrapped up somewhere around the twentieth point, Archie having scored all but three of them. I watched Eric climb out of the pool, my eyes dipping down to where his shorts clung to his shape. *All* of his shape. He peeled the shorts off his skin and walked my way, his entire package in full swing.

Jesus, the things I want to do to that man.

Which I won't do. Because it's not allowed.

The sliding glass door opened just as Eric walked past it. My sister and her boyfriend stepped out, both of them looking ready to jump in the pool. I gave them a wave, which made Eric turn and look over his shoulder.

He froze. Cocked his head.

"Jax?"

"Eric?"

I stood up, water splashing around my feet as I stepped out onto the hot stone floor.

"*Jackson Miller?*" Eric asked again, sounding completely surprised.

I cut in before the sequence could continue. "You two know each other?" I blinked through the surprise, looking at a genuinely shocked Eric and a slightly amused Jax.

Shit... was this going to fuck up our plans?

17

ERIC RUIZ

JACKSON MILLER, a man with a vicious smile and a penchant for holding grudges. I had worked a case years ago, back when I'd first started my career as a PI, and it had involved one of his clients. Someone accused of stealing hundreds of thousands of dollars from a close relative. I discovered the trail of money leading right back to his client's doorstep and got him thrown in jail.

Jackson appeared to have taken that personally, going on a rampage to try and take me out of business. Whether through fake online reviews I had to work to take down or through trying to get my license revoked, one way or another, he had been determined to make me pay, and he had failed with every desperate measure he took.

"Yeah, we've got history," I said to Colton's question about us knowing each other.

I couldn't believe it. *He* was Amelia's lawyer? And now her daughter's boyfriend?

No, wait. There was a ring on his hand. Colton must have noticed it, too, pointing at the silver band.

"Hold up," he said, cocking his head to look at Kendall's left hand. She lifted it and wiggled her finger.

"He did it at the airport, on the way here." She bounced up and down, giving a rogue squeal that matched Colton's as he took her into a hug.

Wow, he's petty and romantic as a pet rock. What a catch.

"Congrats, you guys."

"Congratulations," I managed to say. The shock of this meeting was starting to wear off.

"Okay, but can we go back to you guys knowing each other?" Colton asked with a finger wagging between Jax and me. This wasn't exactly the right time to dive into that, so I shot Colton a look that I hoped would stop any further questioning.

Jax—who either didn't notice the look or didn't care—went ahead with a bullshit explanation about us having worked together a few years ago. Which was rich, considering this was the man who had tried to put me out of business.

Colton didn't seem to be buying it. He arched his brow but didn't chase it any further. Kendall must have sensed some awkward tension because she looped her arm through Jax's and pulled him over to the pool, where the rest of the family was curiously eyeing the newcomers.

"What the hell was that about?" Colton asked in a

low voice. We walked over to the covered patio, where a bevy of lounge chairs was arranged around a smooth stone fire pit. Colton sat down, patting the beige seat next to him.

"We've crossed paths before, but it wasn't as friendly as Jax is making it seem." I took a seat next to Colton, filling him in on the situation while keeping an eye on the dynamics of the group. It seemed like Archie wasn't too happy about Jax being here, either. He gave him a quick handshake and swam to the far end of the pool, where Wendy sat with her feet in the water. She didn't even bother getting up to say hi to them, and her congratulations on the proposal seemed as dry as a desert.

"Did anyone know your sister was dating your mom's lawyer?"

Colton shook his head, sitting back, his legs open wide and his palm-tree-covered shorts riding up his muscular thighs. Normally someone man-spreading (or splaining, for that matter) got on my last fucking nerve, but with Colton, I didn't mind at all.

"It's a shock to all of us. Along with that proposal. She mentioned she was bringing someone and that we knew them, but she never said a name."

"Interesting," I said, watching as Kendall and Jax rolled their suitcases to the side and went over to stand by Jen, who seemed to be the most enthusiastic about their marital news.

"Have your dad or grandma gotten here yet?"

"Nope," Colton said. "Just us kids for now. Well, and our little brother, Archie."

Archie Cooper, the math and tech savant along with being a family prodigy. He had seemed poised to take over his mother's business, trained in her shadow from the moment he could read and write. From social media, it seemed like he was a huge momma's boy, always posting tributes to her and attending nearly every gala, event, and award ceremony his mother had been invited to.

Until his gambling and drug addiction got the best of him and he nearly lost it all. Colton filled me in on that dark period, when Archie went on a complete bender, pushing everyone away and losing all of his money. His mom bailed him out, and after a successful stint in rehab, he was able to fight off his demons and successfully open up his own company.

I stood up, figuring it was as good a time as any. "I'm going to do some snooping around. Do you want to come along and be my lookout?"

Colton's eyebrows jerked up his forehead. A smile crept onto his face. God, he looked like a modern-day James Dean. Casually cool with an effortless smolder to him, highlighted by golden hair and smooth skin that glowed under the cloudless French sky. He looked like a god amongst men, and all I wanted to do was kiss him.

Too bad we already were halfway to our limit.

"Let's go," he said, standing up and holding two fingers in the air, his hands pressed together. "I've always wanted to be a spy."

"Relax, Mr. Smith. I just want to do some light digging."

"You got it, Mrs. Smith." He shot me a wink and turned toward the home. "We're going to go get freshened up for dinner," Colton announced to the group. The sounds of splashing and music nearly disappeared as we entered the living room and shut the thick glass door behind us.

"Alright, let's be quick about this. Do you know who's staying in which rooms?"

"Yup, come this way. Kendall's supposed to be staying in this one." He looked over his shoulder and wiggled the door handle, finding it unlocked. He pushed it open and tiptoed inside. I walked in past him, going straight for the book bag on the shining marble floor. There was a long window above the expensive leather headboard that looked out to the side of the property, away from the pool.

"What are we looking for?" Colton asked, opening a drawer before immediately closing it.

"You need to stand by the door and tell me if anyone's coming. I'm looking for anything that might seem a little off... like this." I pulled out a Hermès wallet from inside the book bag. "Since when can your sister afford a thousand-dollar wallet?"

"Maybe Jax got it for her?" Colton asked as he leaned into the hall.

"Maybe," I said, not finding anything else in the backpack besides a couple of books and a nearly empty bottle of Xanax. I moved to the other side of the bed, where it appeared Jax had left his suitcase open and on the floor. I crouched down, not seeing anything except a bunch of colorful underwear and terribly folded shirts, until a glint of silver and blue caught my eye. A watch, an expensive one.

"Jax has a Rolex, just tossed in casually with his underwear. Does he really make that much money as a lawyer?"

I looked up as Colton shrugged, his back to me as he kept a lookout—his bare, muscular, slightly damp back. Lines slithered and curved up and around his shoulder blades, trailing down his spine, highlighting a column of pure muscle.

Nothing else caught my attention in the suitcase. I stood up, about to move on to the next room, when Colton made a sound.

"What? Someone coming?"

He shook his head, eyes locked on something in Jax's suitcase. "No, I'm just wondering why Jax has that necklace. It's one of the necklaces our mom gave us. Just the kids. It has her initials with ours intertwined at the front... see? It's Kendall's."

"Really? Maybe they just packed together?"

Colton's eyes narrowed. I could always tell when Colton clicked into his overthinking mode. Wrinkles would appear in his forehead, and his eyebrows inched together, his tongue peeking out the side of his mouth.

"Come, let's check out the next room," I said, grabbing his hand and quickly releasing it. Fake. We were supposed to be fake. Holding hands in private wasn't something fake boyfriends did.

"Wait," Colton said, grabbing my hand and spinning

me around to face him, fingers slipping through mine. He didn't let go, and I didn't pull away from him.

He licked his lips, his blue eyes locking me in place. "I'm glad you're here."

"I'm glad, too," I said, my heart starting to pick up its pace. I could smell some of the salt water from the pool still on him, mixing with the coconut-scented sunblock he used.

Fake. We were supposed to be fake.

But... well, fuck it.

I went in for a kiss at the same time he did, our lips locking in a much more passionate kiss than the one I had gotten when I'd first arrived. His tongue slipped past my lips and swirled around mine, giving me a taste of him. I moaned. Couldn't help it. Holding him against me, feeling him getting hard with only a couple threads of fabric separating us, it burned away any idea of this being a fake relationship.

A sound made us freeze. Voices. They were growing louder, coming from down the hall.

"Shit," I said, frustrated that not only did I get distracted but also that this fiery kiss was now being interrupted. "Let's get out of here."

I walked with Colton out of the bedroom, holding his hand, just as three people turned the corner, their suitcases rolling loudly behind them as if announcing the new arrivals.

"Pop, Grams," Colton said, waving as we headed toward the smiling trio.

Well, looked like I was meeting his dad and grand-mother with the taste of Colton still on my lips.

18

COLTON COOPER

GRANDMA MACY CAME OVER and wrapped me up in one of her famous bear hugs. For an eighty-year-old woman, she had a surprising amount of upper-body strength. I sucked in a breath as I felt a couple of pops in my back and shoulders. She smelled like lavender, her favorite scent, as she planted a kiss on each of my cheeks.

"I have to do it the French way," she said with a wink, stepping aside and being replaced by my dad.

His hugs were a little less enthusiastic but still welcome all the same. "Hey, Dad." I bounced from him to Luna, who also gave me two kisses and a warm shoulder squeeze.

"And who's this handsome gentleman?" Macy asked, lowering the designer sunglasses that were likely prescription and made specifically for her.

She was likely the reason why my mom had been such a successful and powerful businesswoman. My grandmother, Macy, had her own thriving business long before my mother hired her first employee. She'd moved here from Greece when she was only fourteen years old and was a well-known name in the fashion world by the time she was twenty-seven. She had her own line of high-end clothes that made it into all the exclusive storefront windows and runways, designing for red carpets and movie premieres, often getting us a couple of free tickets.

She was an inspiration, and we all looked up to her.

"This is Eric," I said, introducing my "boyfriend" with a hand on his lower back.

"Nice to meet you, Eric." Macy came in for a hug while my dad offered a handshake instead.

I noticed he was looking much better than the last time I'd seen him. Granted, it was at mom's funeral, so he had plenty of reason to look shaken and disheveled, but it was good to see him smiling and freshly shaved again, with a sharp haircut and clothes that weren't wrinkled and smelling like wet laundry.

"Well, we're going to get ready for dinner. We'll see you guys later."

"Great meeting you," Eric offered to the group, his dimples on full display. It was the kind of smile that—if properly harnessed—could solve world hunger and climate change all in one go. It was that powerful, that pure, that damn handsome. I lov—nope. Not going down that road. I had already broken our rules once today. I couldn't feel this warm and this excited and this damn giddy every time I looked at him.

I couldn't allow myself to get hurt again. Nope. Not doing it.

I started down the hall, leaving Eric to fend for himself. I heard him say another set of goodbyes before following behind me. We didn't speak, the silence almost suffocating. I got in the shower and played some music to try and change the mood, but not even Bad Bunny could salvage this mess.

THE SILENCE BROKE SOMETIME after Eric's shower, when we were almost done getting ready.

"Everything's okay, right?" Eric asked as he ran some gel through his hair. We were in the bathroom, steam still clouding the air from Eric's apparently burning hot shower.

"Yeah, no, everything's fine. Why?"

"Because you've been giving me the cold shoulder after we kissed that last time."

"I have?" I asked, knowing damn well that I had.

"I mean, unless I'm imagining it. I just want to make sure I'm not doing anything to upset you, that's all."

We locked eyes in the foggy mirror. It was a large bathroom, with two sinks spaced feet apart from each other. The mirror had a built-in light that made it look as if we were filming a skin-care routine for a national brand. "I'm not upset. I'm just... thrown. That's all."

"We can slow things down. Add some more rules." He looked like a scolded puppy. It warmed my heart to see how much he cared about me, which only made me more annoyed.

Couldn't you care this much about me back when you were pushing me out of your apartment?

"I think the rules we have now are fine. I just have to adjust to being here, being with you, being without my—" I choked on the word, unable to say it. I looked at myself in the mirror, surprised. I wasn't expecting these kinds of emotions, but the storm clouds rolled in without a second's warning. Thunder clapped in my chest. I swallowed a lump of rocks and wiped at my cheek.

Eric reached across the small chasm that had formed between us. His hand on my shoulder was a welcome touch. "We're here for her," Eric said. "Just remember that."

I nod, which quickly morphed into a head shake. "Which also means we're suspecting someone in this villa of orchestrating her death. So fucking fucked-up." The sink was cold as my fingers clasped around the edge of it. Eric's hand moved from my shoulder to my lower back, the trail of warmth fighting against the icy-cold dread and gloom currently setting up residence inside of me.

I turned on the cold water and pooled some in my hand, splashing it on my face before turning off the faucet. "It's fine," I said, sounding more like I was trying to convince myself than Eric. "Let's just go to dinner. I'm sure everyone's seated already."

Eric glanced at his watch. "It's only five thirty. Isn't dinner at seven?"

"Yeah, but my family's weird, as you can already tell." I spritzed myself with a dash of cologne and left Eric in the bathroom, slipping on some socks and then my sneakers just as Eric walked into the room, his hair perfectly done and his black button-up shirt perfectly pressed and his dimples perfectly framing that perfect smile of his.

"Ready," he said, hands casually in the pockets of his dark jeans.

I got off the bed and turned my back to him, trying to break whatever spell he had cast on me. "Let's go."

The spell didn't break. Not even with Eric walking three steps behind me. I still wanted to turn around and throw him against the wall, kissing him in a way that made this *real*. I wanted to kiss him and to hold him and to make him feel how badly I wanted him.

Thankfully, he didn't ask me why I appeared to be running from some kind of demon because I wasn't entirely sure I even had an excuse this time.

We were the last ones to make it to the dinner table, just like I had said. My entire family was already sitting around the long table, wine poured and bread placed on tiny plates. The villa had come with a private chef, who was just walking into the room with a tray of appetizers as I took my seat next to Jen.

The dining room had a sliding glass wall that opened up to the yard, so on days with good weather (like today), it was like we were eating outside with the French Alps as our dinner guests. A gentle breeze rolled in and made the silk white table runner shift and dance underneath the vibrant bouquet made of pastel pink roses, sunshine-yellow sunflowers, and long stalks of lavender.

My mom's three favorite flowers.

"Eric, is this your first time in France?" Jen asked as she leaned over me to grab some of the bacon-wrapped dates the chef had just placed on the table.

"It is, it is."

"Enjoying it so far?" my dad asked, effortlessly sliding into the conversation. He sat at the head of the table, looking relaxed in a light blue polo shirt, the sleeves rolled and the buttons on the collar left open.

"I am. This feels like being dropped into a storybook."

"It does, doesn't it? Amelia and I had our first vacation with the kids here, and from that summer on, it became a tradition of sorts. It's too bad this is the last year we get to do this."

"I still don't see the need to sell this place," Matthew said, looking around at the open-air dining room, his gaze full of the same memories that flicked across my brain. Running through this very room as kids playing freeze tag, coming here after Matt's high school graduation, spending Jen's fifteenth birthday here, me coming out to my family in the yard.

So many memories, and all of them more special than the last.

"It just makes sense," Dad said in a tone that implied he didn't want to talk about it anymore.

Archie didn't seem to mind. He swirled his glass of red wine and took a gulp. I noticed there was a dark purple tint to his lips, meaning this wasn't his first glass, and I had a feeling it wouldn't be his last, either. As if reading my mind, he grabbed the bottle of red wine from off the table and gave himself a healthy pour, the glug-glug of the wine leaving the bottle seeming to echo around the now quiet room.

"So, Jax," Archie said, his hands making a loose fist on the table. There was a twist to his tone, a sneer on his face, that told me something had shifted. "When are you going to read the will?"

The tension wound around the table like a hungry python. My lungs felt tight as the air was sucked out of the room. It was partly why we were all there, and the sooner we got it over with, the better, but it was still difficult to even think about, much less talk about.

"I discussed that with your father, and he agreed that waiting until the end of our stay here would be best."

I sat up stiffly in my chair. That wasn't what I expected to hear, and judging by the surprised faces around me, I wasn't the only one.

"Seriously?" Matt said, his fork clinking against his plate. "Shouldn't we just read it as soon as possible?"

I noticed Kendall wasn't reacting, her eyes glued to her lap. He must have told her already. Perks of dating the family lawyer, I guess.

"Matt," my dad said, putting a hand out and grabbing my brother's wrist. "Let's just enjoy these two weeks. We won't have this villa after this year, and it was your mom's favorite escape. I'm sure she was fair and compassionate with whatever she left behind, so let's not worry about it until the end of this trip, okay?"

Matt looked like he was about to argue. He and dad always butted heads, but it was rare that Matt would win any of those battles, and he seemed to have recognized that tonight. He sat back, picking up his fork and going back to eating.

"Is that why you're doing it?" Archie asked, looking across the table at Jax. Behind him, the sun was beginning to set on the distant mountains, draping them in a tapestry of orange and purple.

Matthew may not have been confrontational, but Archie surely was. "Or is there another reason?" he asked, leaning forward.

"What are you talking about?" Jax looked as confused as I felt.

"Are you holding off on reading it because your name is on it, too? Scared someone here is going to be upset by that?" Archie crossed his arms, cocking his head, his purple lips twisting into a sneer.

"Why would his name be on it?" Jen asked.

"Yeah, Jax, why *would* your name be on it?" Archie prodded. I wasn't catching on to whatever he was tossing out. I looked at Eric from the side of my eye. His expression was neutral, but his gaze was locked on Jax, as if analyzing the tiniest of micro-movements in the man's face.

"I don't think I follow," Jax said, sitting back in his chair. He gave the impression of someone sitting in an uncomfortably hot sauna, shifting and tugging at his shirt.

"Really?"

"Archie," Wendy said, a hand on her husband's. She gave him a look that my brother completely ignored.

"So you're going to completely ignore the fact that

you were in a relationship with my mom for years before you got with my sister?"

A gasp sounded from the table, but I wasn't sure who it had come from. Maybe me?

"Is that true?" my dad asked.

"We aren't doing this right now," Kendall said, taking the napkin off her lap and moving to stand up.

"No, wait," Jax said. She sat back, holding onto the balled up napkin in tight fists. He closed his eyes and rubbed at the bridge of his nose. "Yes... it is true," Jackson said to the resounding surprise of everyone sitting at the dinner table. "Amelia and I did date. For about three years."

My jaw dropped. "Three years? How did we not hear about this?" I asked.

"We were both content on keeping things quiet. My family situation was complicated, and hers was as well."

Archie's expression twisted into something that looked like disdain as he stared at Kendall. Wendy mirrored her husband, down to the same eyebrow wrinkle and twisted grimace. "Out of everyone you could be dating, you decide to date him? How dare you disrespect Mom's memory like that."

Kendall looked like she had been slapped across the face. She huffed out a breath, fidgeting with a hairband on her wrist as she looked for words. I braced myself. Fights between Archie and Kendall never ended well.

"How did you even know?" Kendall asked, looking as if she were ready to launch herself across the table at Archie.

"That doesn't matter." He turned his focus back to Jax. "What really matters is how you can go to sleep at night next to him, knowing he's been with Mom."

The table got deathly silent. As if someone had dropped a thick curtain on the scene, turning off the stage lights and plunging the theatre into quiet. I gritted my teeth, reaching for Eric's hand under the table and giving him a squeeze. I could tell he was equally as shocked by my sister's outburst as I was, but he didn't know how much worse it could really get.

I did. I had seen my sister flip into one of her rage-filled modes before. It never turned out well.

"You all want to judge, you all want to point fingers. Except you're all just equally full of shit," she spat, leaning forward. "Archie, how many times did you steal from Mom to support your gambling addiction, huh? And Matt, the golden child of the family, when are you going to tell Dad that you're the reason he and Mom split, huh?"

My father's head whipped as if on a swivel, turning to his left and looking at a paper-pale Matthew. My brother was never good with confrontation, always locking himself in a room at the slightest sign of a fight. It looked like he was seconds away from hiding under the table until we were all gone.

"Is that true?" my dad asked, voice shaking.

"I—she asked me. She told me, actually, that she wasn't happy. I'd noticed how you two had changed, how there weren't any more date nights or random kisses and hugs. I just mentioned that maybe she needed some time alone. I just meant she needed to think things over. I was a junior in high school—what the hell was I supposed to say?"

"Three days later, Mom served you the divorce papers." Kendall looked proud of herself. She had always loved to play with fire, and now she sat back down and watched as the dinner table caught ablaze with the match she had tossed.

"Why did you never tell me this?"

Matt shook his head and mouthed words that didn't materialize. He looked like a fish gasping for breath. "I don't think this is the right time," I cut in, wanting to throw my brother a life raft. He didn't deserve this. Kendall had flipped it all around, taking attention away from Jax and throwing Matt, her own brother, into the fire.

Shit. This dinner was turning out to be an absolute fucking nightmare, and the main course hadn't even been brought out yet.

19

ERIC RUIZ

THIS WAS QUICKLY DETERIORATING. Like watching a nuclear reactor melting down in real time. The clock that ticked down toward pure annihilation was right there on William's face, growing redder by each passing second, matching the red plates the chef and his helpers placed down on the table, each plate with a mouthwatering steak sitting on grilled asparagus and a swirl of what appeared to be dark chocolate. Kendall was back in her seat but her temper was still clearly flaring.

"And here we have our filets mignons imported from New Zealand, cooked over a thyme and basil reduction with a spicy chocolate drizzle. Enjoy."

The chef bowed his head and left, seemingly oblivious to the war zone he had just evacuated from.

"Why, Matt?"

"I was young. I told her what I felt. I didn't think—it wasn't my fault. I didn't force her to leave you."

Krystine looked to her boyfriend with sympathetic eyes. She reached out a hand and placed it on his. Matthew didn't seem to notice.

"But you planted the seed. Against your own father." He leaned back in the chair, eyes drilling a hole directly through Matt's chest. He looked hurt, but the anger seemed to be simmering under something else. Disappointment?

Archie sat up, drawing attention to him. "No, don't let Kendall do that. She's not flipping this around. Not when the person who needs to be explaining themselves is sitting right there." He looked to Jax, who was cutting his steak and taking a bite, shutting his eyes as he chewed. Blood mixed with the swirls of dark chocolate.

"Wow, that is *good.*" He looked around the table as if surprised none of us were eating. "What? What do you want me to do here, Archie? Break up with your sister?"

Archie shook his head and narrowed his eyes. He looked ready to drop another bomb. "Matt wasn't the reason Mom asked for a divorce, is it?"

Kendall shot to her feet, pushing her chair back and tossing her napkin onto the table. "We aren't doing this. It's our first day here—I'm not sitting through this."

"What is he talking about?" Jen asked. Macy and Luna were watching from the corner of the table in silence, grim expressions on both of their faces. Luna fiddled with a rainbow-colored bracelet, spinning the beads around her skinny wrist.

"Maybe this isn't the best time," Wendy said with a hand on her husband's back, her brown eyes full of worry and warning. I tried to clock every look, every tiny move and facial expression. This dinner may have been taking a turn for the worst, but it was also presenting a chance to observe Colton's family in a way that wouldn't be possible if we were just talking about the weather. Tension and anger normally brought out hard truths that would otherwise have remained buried, whether intentionally or not. It also allowed me to see who had the hottest temper and who sitting at this very table could be capable of being behind Amelia's death.

Kendall spoke before Jax could, pulling him up onto his feet. "This isn't going down tonight. Come on, Jax. We can go somewhere else for dinner."

"No," Colton's dad said. The single word cut through the room with the force of a bullet slamming through the wall. "We discuss this tonight. What is Archie talking about?"

"Dad." Kendall had an almost pleading look in her eyes. "Please."

I looked to Colton, who had been silent for a majority of this. He had his eyes glued to Jax, sitting directly across from him. I remembered him telling me his family dynamics were complicated back when we had first met, but I didn't imagine it ever being this bad.

It'd been around Thanksgiving time, and I had asked him if he was going back home. We'd already been hooking up in secret for a month at that point. When he told me he was thinking of staying, I'd immediately extended him an invite to dinner with my family. No one questioned it when I brought my friend from the police academy to eat with us, although looking back on it, I wondered if my mom knew what was really going on between Colton and me. She had been extra vocal about how much she loved me that night.

"Amelia and I—yes, we got together around the time of her divorce. Her divorce attorney was a close friend of mine. I was visiting her office the same day Amelia came in to file. We bumped into each other in the elevator, and I just—"

"He's lying," Archie said, his face beginning to match the same shade of red as his father's. They looked very much alike, beyond the anger that colored their cheeks. Same crooked nose, same thin eyebrows, same satellite-like ears. "I know you were seeing my mom weeks before she filed for divorce. You weren't at that office as a coincidence. You were there to support her while you tore our family apart."

"How do you even know any of this? Or are you back to making up lies about people to distract from whatever bullshit is going on in your life? Huh?" Kendall asked, venom dripping from her words. She was framed by the beautiful French countryside stretching out behind her, the sun having already set and the moon taking her place in the star-blotted sky.

Kendall did bring up a good point. How *did* Archie know all of this?

"You know what," Kendall said, fire burning in her eyes. "It doesn't even matter. Come on. Let's go. And Archie, little brother, maybe you should worry about your failing business before you worry about us, okay?"

She grabbed Jax by the elbow and tugged him up onto his feet. He grabbed his glass of wine and made a wordless exit with his girlfriend, the sound of her heels stomping on the stone following them back into the villa. They shut the heavy glass door, which was when Kendall must have started to yell, her voice muffled and getting lower as they went back to their bedroom.

"Jesus," Colton said. He formed a loose fist with his hands and put them up to his mouth. I reached for his leg under the table and gave his thigh a supportive squeeze. I wasn't sure if that crossed some unwritten rule in our arrangement; it just felt like the right thing to do in that moment. This wasn't easy by any stretch of the imagination.

Colton's father shook his head and huffed out a breath before he bundled up his napkin and set it next to his plate, his steak untouched. "Tell the chef I thank him for the meal and I'm sorry I can't eat right now." He got up and disappeared down the hallway, his footsteps loud as he stomped up the stairs.

"What a fucking joke." Archie mirrored his father by throwing the napkin on the table and rising up onto his feet, Wendy following him as he went down the opposite hallway, the two of them silent as they went to their bedroom.

That left Jen, Colton, Macy, and Luna at the table. Luna looked stunned as she took off her glasses and let them hang around her neck, running a hand through her white-and-gray curls.

Macy clicked her tongue and looked to her wife. "I

warned you, didn't I? My family is crazier than a gaggle of gays at a drag brunch full of bottomless mimosas and topless bottoms."

That outrageous comparison cut through some of the thick tension hanging in the air. Laughter replaced the shouting from just moments before. I could tell Macy had seen quite a bit, being the matriarch of such a large and complex family. She had stayed silent during the arguing, but now she was stepping onto center stage with a story about the time the family vacationed in Sicily and got into it with a traveling clown troupe at a five-star restaurant.

It gave me a different view of Colton and his family. A lighter one. During a time when they were still a functioning unit, supporting each other instead of lunging for each other's throats.

Except for Archie, who was absent from her story. It confirmed what Colton had told me before this trip: Archie had been the black sheep of the family at some point, being the only one missing. It must have been during his battle with addiction, which he appeared to have fought off successfully. Nothing about him in his current state told me he was back on drugs or gambling, but sometimes vices were as invisible as the damage they slowly incurred, until it was far too late to intervene.

The five of us managed to retain our appetite and finish off the meal. I tried to dig for some more information on the family dynamics, but it seemed like the table wanted to move on to other topics. I didn't press, although I did have some new questions forming that needed answers.

Was Jackson really the cause of Amelia and William's divorce?

How did Archie know so much about Jax?

Did Kendall know Jackson had been dating her mom?

And did any of it have to do with Amelia's untimely death? I had gone into this thinking money was the prime motive behind a possible murder, but could it be something else?

By the time the chef took our plates, the mood had considerably shifted. Macy had a way of pulling in everyone around her with her animated storytelling, assisted by a couple of funny asides from Luna. They were like a practiced act, bouncing off each other, elevating one another. It was fun to watch and left me with a sore stomach from laughing so hard.

"Alright, it's been fun, you all, but Luna and I need to get our beauty sleep. This jet lag is slapping us across the face and calling us Sally."

"Which is actually my middle name," Luna said cheerily as they stood up.

"And here I was thinking your middle name was Tuna this entire time."

Luna shot Macy a glare that nearly tipped her off. "Only because you insist on calling me Luna Tuna, as if being compared to a stinky fish is some kind of cutesy compliment."

"It's better than Luna from the Black Lagoona."

Macy put her arms up and pretended she was some kind of zombie creature, grabbing Luna in her arms and kissing her cheek. It was heartwarming to watch the way Luna's eyes lit up at Macy's touch. They clearly loved each other, which made me wonder about their entire story. When and how did they meet? Was it this late in life, or had they known each other years earlier, only pursuing something now that the time felt right?

Like Colton and me... except they were the furthest thing from "fake" as could be.

"You guys headed to bed, too?" Jen asked before finishing the last of her wine.

"Yeah, but not to sleep," Colton said.

Jen's eyebrows shot up, and a surprised sound came from my throat before I realized what Colton had meant. His cheeks instantly got cherry red as he jumped to clarify. "We've got a book club meeting we're staying up for. Get your heads out of the gutter."

"*Riiiiight,*" Jen said. "Is that what the kids are calling it these days?"

She got up with a chuckle and waved over her shoulder. "Night, boys. Have fun reading or whatever."

Colton shook his head and rolled his eyes, cheeks still a bright pink. It was so fucking cute. I wanted to lean in and kiss him, press my lips against that warm and flushed skin. But I'd already gotten my limit of kisses today, and I didn't want to press any further. Not after the whirlwind of a night we'd just had.

I decided to control myself, getting up from the table and following Colton as we went to our room, neither of us speaking much. He was likely still processing the conversations that were had at the dinner table while I was scanning every inch of the villa as we walked through it, trying to spot anything that could help with this case.

In one of the living rooms was where I noticed a couple of black bags sitting on the couch, a company logo emblazoned across the center of them.

AC Tech and Security.

I stopped Colton with a gentle hand on his elbow. "Whose are those?" I asked, not surprised to see that Amelia had raised other entrepreneurs in her family.

"That's Archie's tech company. They sell stuff and help fix things, too. They also pride themselves on delivering items straight to your house and installing them for you. It's a hit with the older crowd, for sure."

"When did he start it?"

Colton chewed on his cheek and quirked his lip. "Couple of years ago. Once he got out of rehab for the third time. I guess it really was a charm." Colton glanced at his wristwatch. "We've got thirty minutes until the Zoom call. That's enough time to freshen up and mindlessly scroll through TikTok for a little bit."

"Let's go," I said, wordlessly filing away the tidbit of Archie's business in my mental case files. I'd have to look into it a little further, but for now, I had other things to focus on: like the way Colton's ass jiggled on his way up the stairs. That kept my entire attention as we climbed the spiraling staircase, giving me a semi by the time we reached the landing, which I adjusted with a hand in my pocket so that it was held down by my waistband as I grew harder, my mind wandering in directions that weren't allowed but were very much wanted.

Damn it, Colton. If this is supposed to be fake, then why does it feel so fucking real?

20

COLTON COOPER

WE WERE LYING IN BED, waiting for the start of the book club. With the time difference, we had decided that midnight our time would probably work best. There were twenty minutes left, which the two of us filled by scrolling through our phones, chuckling at viral videos and memes, leaning over to show one another when it was a particularly funny one. It was a good way to scrub the brain after the shitshow we'd just had to sit through at dinner.

Jackson and my mom? The reason for my parents' divorce? And now he was with my sister, here at this retreat, holding the last will and testament of the woman we all apparently loved.

How in the hell did that happen? And did it have anything to do with her death?

There were a thousand questions storming through my brain, rattling around without any accompanying answers. And none of them were being answered by the cutesy viral dance that kept popping up on my timeline. I was about to close out of the app when another swipe brought up a thirst trap video, showing a particularly hunky guy climbing out of a pool with his wet shorts clinging to his body for dear life. There was a clear outline at the front that made me suddenly want to go take a dip in the pool myself.

I swiped up, the algorithm apparently just as horny as I was, another video of a half-naked man chopping wood filling up my screen. His grunts and muscles were doing it for me. I crossed my feet at the ankles and readjusted myself, wondering if my growing bulge wasn't all that obvious. I glanced to my left, seeing Eric smiling at whatever funny thing had just landed on his phone. I swallowed.

We were both on the bed together, only inches separating us. There wasn't a pillow barrier or a comforter wall between us. I could easily kick my leg to the side and cross it with his, our bare feet rubbing together. My briefs got even tighter. I turned my attention back to the phone and swiped up.

Next was a video of a guy getting off a bike with a massive bulge in his cycling suit.

Gah damn, what is going on with this app?

I double-tapped it with one hand and moved my boner with the other. I was wearing a pair of black sweats that helped hide the effect these videos were having on me.

Or at least I thought they did.

"You alright there?" Eric asked, looking down at the hand that was cupping my erection.

"I, uh, yeah, totally fine."

"You're just moving around a lot. The bed keeps shifting."

"I'm just getting comfortable."

Eric cocked a brow, smirking. "I can see that." Eric shifted so that his legs opened up a little wider and grabbed himself. My eyes shot down to the tent that now formed in his blue shorts. "I noticed you were getting excited, which got me all worked up."

I licked my lips, eyes going back to my screen. This wasn't good. "We don't have any rules set up for when we get hard at the same time while lying in bed and watching dumb videos."

"Let's make a rule right now then: we get to watch each other jerk off. But we don't touch each other. Just to keep things, you know, fake."

There were plenty of reasons why this was a bad idea. It made things between us even more complicated. It reminded me of the time we spent in the academy together.

It made me want to do more than just watch.

But I couldn't think properly past the throbbing of my cock. I *wanted* to watch Eric stroke himself. I *wanted* to be reminded of our time together.

"Fine," I said, rubbing myself through my sweats. "But no touching. And this only happens tonight."

"Deal."

Eric pulled off his shorts, kicking them off the bed and leaving him in just a pair of gray briefs. He was rock hard. The fabric of his briefs was darkening around the head of his cock, telling me just how excited this arrangement made him. I licked my lips and stopped myself from reaching over. I instead focused on myself, lifting my butt and pulling off my sweatpants, my stiff cock springing free.

"I knew you weren't wearing any underwear," Eric said, his eyes glued to my pulsing dick.

"Alright, your turn." I motion with my chin at his briefs, which looked like they were two dick twitches away from tearing apart. Eric smiled as he took them off, leaving us both naked from the waist down. I took a moment to admire how fucking sexy this man was, with his beer-can-thick cock and dark crown of bushy hair, a few veins running up his shaft. A drop of clear precum oozed from his slit. He rubbed his thumb over it, lifting his thumb to show a connected string shining in the bright light of the bedroom.

I stretched out in the bed, spitting in my hand and slowly rubbing it over myself. He pointed at my phone. "Go ahead," he said, "Put something on for us to watch."

I licked my lips, smiling, my heart pumping faster than usual. I'd never watched porn with someone else before. It always felt like something private, almost more intimate than sex itself. Only because it was so secretive, even though it was something I'd venture to say ninety-nine percent of humankind consumed at one point or another. What if Eric didn't like the kind of videos I enjoyed? Would he judge me? Or would he want something less vanilla than the things I watched?

"You first," I said, suddenly feeling a bout of nerves.

He didn't miss a beat, grabbing his phone and switching over to his web browser's incognito mode. He typed in a website and tapped on a video, the screen filling with a handsome Latin guy sitting back on a leather couch, legs open with a tattooed twink kneeling between them, both his hands wrapped around the Latin guy's thick cock.

Eric propped the phone up on a pillow between us. "That okay?" he asked, already jerking himself off.

"Yeah, that's really hot." I looked at the screen, watching as the cameraman moved in closer, highlighting just how big of a cock the guy on the couch had. From my periphery, I could see Eric's closed fist gliding up and down his cock. I looked over at him, watching as he massaged his balls. I noticed he was looking at me, both of us ignoring the struggling twink as he tried to get that behemoth of a penis down his throat.

The room was getting hot, the air turning to steam. I looked back to the screen, the twink somehow managing to unhinge his jaw and get a couple of inches in his mouth. "That's a huge dick," I said, gripping my own in a loose fist. "Ever been with one that big?"

"I have. I bottomed for the first time with a dick that big, actually."

I quickened my strokes. The combination of the video, the sounds coming from it, and the rumble of Eric's voice as he spoke about getting fucked for the first time—it made me overheat, flames licking up my sides and spreading through me as if my blood had been swapped with motor oil.

"I thought you were strictly a top?"

He chuckled, slapping his hard cock against his open palm. I curled my toes and rubbed on my tightening balls. "I mostly top, but I can't be letting you bottoms have all the P-spot fun, can I? Something about being on my fours with a hard dick sliding in and out of me drives me fucking feral."

God damn it. It took everything I had to stick to the boundaries we set up. I knew, just fucking knew, that if I reached over and held him in my hands, if I jerked him off until he shot his load, I'd only fall harder for him. Harder than I was already falling.

Fallen.

"*Fuuuck*," I said in a hiss, dropping my head onto the cushioned headrest and closing my eyes.

"Getting close?" Eric asked, his voice low. I could almost feel his breath against my skin. Or was I imagining that? The way I imagined his hand stroking my cock instead of my own.

I nodded, jerking off a little harder, applying more pressure. The sounds of both our fists slapping against skin competed with the gurgling sounds coming from Eric's phone. I opened my eyes, seeing that the twink had managed to get nearly half of the dick down his throat before he had to come up gasping for air.

I looked to Eric's rock-hard cock. He had his feet touching, legs open as if in a stretch.

"Do it, Colt. I want to see you nut."

It was all I needed. As if Eric stood behind me on the cliff, pushing me off it with his words alone. I came all over my shirt, my legs kicking out as my balls emptied themselves with shot after shot of cum. As my orgasm subsided, Eric's took over. He announced it with a grunt. His body stiffened as his cock exploded with ropes of his seed.

"Ohh, fuck," I said, watching as he released, his eyes shut and his grip tight around the base of his pulsing cock. The cum slowed to a dribble, sliding down the side of his knuckles and shaft.

I dropped my head back onto the headboard, chuckling, the porn still playing between us. Eric picked up his phone and turned the video off, laughing like I was.

"Damn," he said as he got up from the bed. He took off his shirt in a way that kept most of the cum off him. "That was fun."

"Fun is putting it lightly." I stole a glance at Eric before he disappeared into the bathroom. He was so fucking sexy. He had a furry chest with some hair trailing down and over his belly, making me want to rub my hands all over him. He walked away and gave me a view of that fuzzy peach-shaped ass of his, jiggling as he crossed the bedroom.

Well... I was hard again.

Thankfully, my body calmed down by the time Eric came back from the bathroom, which happened to be just as the clock struck twelve and my phone buzzed with a notification about a Zoom invite.

"Book club time," I said, dressed and feeling like a million bucks, the book on my lap and an easy smile on my face.

21

ERIC RUIZ

I FLOATED ON CLOUD NINE.

The mattress must have been secretly swapped off for a cloud in the time I'd spent washing up and coming back out of the bathroom. I'd never come so hard by just using my hand, but being watched by Colton had made jerking off that much hotter, especially since he was stroking himself at the same time. And best of all, neither of us broke any rules in the process. As badly as I wanted to run my tongue up and down his hard shaft, I somehow managed to keep all hands and feet (and lips) to myself.

Back in the spacious bedroom, I grabbed my iPad and set it up on the desk that looked out of an arching window, the heavy beige curtains drawn shut. A hanging planter was tucked into the corner of the room, some of the emerald-green leaves trailing down all the way to the sturdy desk. Colton grabbed a chair from the other side of the room and brought it over to the table.

He looked like a Greek god, wearing a colorful tank

top with the sides cut out so that his biceps and obliques were on full display. I could see the V-shaped muscles that curved along his hips and dipped down into the gym shorts he had thrown on. I was reminded of the times we'd just lounge around together in just a pair of basket-ball shorts, our bodies spent after an hours-long sex session...

Damn. I had fucked this all up, hadn't I? If only I wasn't so ashamed of my own sexuality back then, I would never have pushed Colton away, would never have hurt him. None of this "fake" bullshit would have even been necessary. I looked at him as he sat down next to me, wondering what our life could have looked like together. Flashes of laughter and joy blinked across my vision. When I was with Colton, I felt happy. *Truly* happy. In a way I hadn't felt for a long, long time. I had been going through a gray swath of life, with nothing or no one exciting me. Even my job had grown stale over the last few months.

But then Colton bumped into me at that coffee shop, and suddenly, my entire world was blasted in technicolor paint.

"I'm glad I'm here with you," I said, causing him to look at me with some surprise. The Zoom call hadn't started yet, but our faces were already being reflected back at us on the screen. "I know it's not for the best of reasons, but I'm still happy you brought me along with you."

Colton's eyes bounced between mine as if he was searching for something. But what? What was he looking for, and how could I get it for him? Because if he told me he wanted the moon in his lap, I would have found a way to pull it down from the sky for him.

A ding from my iPad interrupted Colton before he could respond. We both looked to the screen, Jake and Noah's faces popping up before Tia and Jess appeared underneath them. Yvette and Tristan weren't far behind. I leaned to the side so that Colton and I were in the center of our square, waving at my friends.

"Everyone got their books?" Noah asked as he adjusted his glasses on his face. He and Jake were cuddled up on the couch together, a plush-looking navy blue blanket covering them both.

"More importantly," Tristan said, raising a glass up to the camera, "everyone got their drinks?"

"Ah crap, we don't have any," Colton said.

"Wait, yes we do." I got up and went over to the dresser, where a minifridge had been tucked inside. I opened it and pulled out two beers, popping them open and handing one over to Colton. "Problem solved."

We gave a little cheers to our Reading Under the Rainbow book club, which had just gone global with Colton and me sitting halfway across the world from the rest of the gang.

Tristan leaned forward, looking straight down the camera. "So, how's your vacation going, boys?"

"It's going well," Colton said. "Besides a little dustup at dinner today, so far, things have been fine."

"Judging by the smiles on both your faces, things have

been a little better than just fine," Tristan said with a smirk.

Damn it. Leave it to one of my best friends to pick up on the post-sex glow that was admittedly hard to hide.

"Alright, alright," I said, lifting up the book and waving it at the group. "Let's get this started. Jess, what's tonight's game?"

Jess was the one leading the discussion tonight, so it had been her responsibility to make the night's drinking game. She had a knack for knowing how to get us all blasted ten minutes into the meeting. "Since we're all over the place today, I figured we can play a game of Where in the World is Carmen Sandiego's Drink? Whenever one of us mentions the name of a place, whether fictional or real, then you've got to drink— *unless* you remember to put on your invisible Carmen Sandiego hat before you say the place." Jess mimed putting a hat on her head with both hands and tipped it forward. "But first, let's go back to your trip to France." She winked underneath her invisible hat. "I actually haven't stopped talking about it with Tia."

"She really hasn't," Tia said, shaking her head but smiling as she took a sip of her wine.

"I just stumbled on an article online—not that I was researching your mom or anything, Colton—but it got me thinking about it and how messed up of a situation it is."

I perked up. "Is this blog called Who's Eating the Rich, by any chance?"

"That's the one," she said. "Of course, we don't have

to talk about it if you're not comfortable, Colton. But... maybe we can help?"

Colton sat up a little straighter. I looked at him, seeing a man who'd been through hell and back and who was still able to smile through all of it. And some of that hell was inflicted by the very person sitting next to him. It hurt me to know that I had hurt him. It was a visceral pain, one that wasn't eased by the presence of friends or alcohol. I hated myself for telling Colton I'd never love him. I was projecting all of my fears and insecurities on the one person who mattered to me. One of the only people on this earth capable of helping me fight off those toxic and self-hating traits. "I don't mind at all," he said, looking to me. "Bumping into Eric felt like it was meant to be for a lot of different reasons, but one of those reasons is—I think—to have met you guys."

Yvette put a hand on her chest. Noah and Jake both audibly "awwed" and cuddled in closer together. Tristan raised his glass. "I'm happy you bumped into Eric, and judging by the way he's looking at you, I think he's pretty happy, too. Cheers to that."

We all clinked our glasses against the webcam, although I tried not to think too much about what Tristan said. Was I really looking at Colton in a certain type of way? We hadn't set up any rules about looking at each other... should we have?

Man, fuck these rules.

I reached over and gave Colton's leg a squeeze. Just a quick touch, but one that seemed to spark something in his gaze. His eyebrows tilted downward, his smile falling for a brief moment.

"Has the will been read yet?" Noah asked.

Colton shook his head. "Dad wants to wait until the end of the trip. But after tonight's dinner, I don't know if that's a great idea. Not after finding out my mom had a secret relationship with the family lawyer, who's now dating my sister."

A collective gasp of surprise was released from the group. Colton nodded, lips pursed. "Yeah, things got messy."

Jake seemed to be the first one who was able to fully recover. He spoke up. "Was the lawyer dating your mom at the time of her death?" His question sounded innocent enough, but the suspicion was still there.

Colton just shrugged. I had already made a mental note to look into that timeline. I planned on taking Jax aside and having a mini interrogation session with the petty lawyer, but I'd have to do it when Kendall wasn't around.

"So no one knows if he's in the will?" Noah asked.

Colton shook his head.

"I mean, it would make the most sense," Noah continued. "If someone outside of the family was the one responsible for it? And if he was dating her at the time, then maybe she mentioned his name going on the will at some point? Do we know how long they were together?"

"All I know is when it started," Colton said, "which must have been when my mom and my dad divorced."

"Someone dating her also would likely know where

the secret cameras are placed," Yvette said, running a hand through her mane of curly brown hair. She was right, of course. Unless Amelia didn't trust Jackson enough to tell him where the cameras were, which also didn't exactly help his case out. I knew the man was capable of some playground bully tactics with the way he tried to take me out of business, but was he also capable of murder, too?

"Well, since we're talking about it, I did a little more research into that missing camera Eric mentioned at our last meeting," Tristan said, leaning back in his seat, sporting a proud grin. "I tracked down the information on the cameras that *were* recovered from the scene of the crime, and it looks like they were installed by a company called AC Tech and Security."

Colton and I both turned to look at each other like our heads had been placed on swivels. That was the same company emblazoned on the bags that sat out front by the door. "That's Archie's company," Colton said.

"Archie?" Tristan asked.

"My brother. He owns a tech company, but he never mentioned being the one who installed the cameras. Unless he just didn't think it was that important. Did he install the hidden nanny cam, too?"

Tristan made a "tsk" sound and shook his head. "Hard to tell. I only know they installed it because I googled for local surveillance companies and found them advertised as one of the top. I called them and made pretend I was at the residence and needed some tech support. The girl on the phone confirmed the cameras were still covered under a warranty program at their store, which let me know they were the ones who installed it."

"Nice job, Tristan," I said, proud of my best friend. He was a successful author who enjoyed nerding out on tech stuff, but I hadn't realized he was also coming after my gig, too. "Want to moonlight as a detective with me?"

"Nah, I'll leave that to you. I can't do a stakeout. I get too bored. Unless it's at Outback. Get it? A stakeout while eating a *steak* at Out—okay, you guys get it."

The group broke down into laughter. Tristan had a way of doing that. If writing didn't work out for him, he could easily make a living as a stand-up comedian. He had the charisma and the intelligence, along with a healthy dose of self-awareness.

Just then, another square appeared in the Zoom call, pushing Colton and me to the side.

"Steve!" I said, surprised but happy to see my neighbor had made it. "Everyone, meet Steve. He's new to Atlanta, so I figured our little book club could be a good way for him to meet some new people."

I had sent him the link to the book club and had gotten a tentative "yes," so I wasn't expecting much. I decided if Steve didn't show up for this one, then I wouldn't bother him with it anymore.

"So sorry I'm late. I had an issue at work."

"No worries, Steve." Jess raised her glass. "Do you have a drink?"

"I thought you were going to ask if I had the book."

"Oh no, I'm talking about the important stuff here,"

she said with a wink before diving into the explanation for her drinking game. The night slowly went back onto the predetermined track, with us discussing the chapters we had read, discovering the body was actually the metrical grandmother who was celebrating her birthday. We uncovered a few motives for who'd killed the grandmother, along with a couple of possible red herrings. I already clocked the killer from the opening pages, but it seemed like the rest of the group was still thrown by a couple of errant clues, so I held on to my theory and watched them throw some around. Colton had gotten the closest to my guess while also getting closer to me, moving his chair so that our elbows touched. At one point, our legs had crossed under the desk, and I left it there, rubbing my foot against his. It was such a simple but intimate touch and one that had me instantly rock hard.

The book club ended soon after. My foot was still on Colton's, and I noticed his shorts were just as tented as mine. "Talking about books excites you, huh?" I teased.

"Yeah, literature gets me rock hard."

"I can see that," I said, looking down at the massive bulge. "We should take care of it."

"We should," Colton said. I opened my web browser, pulling up the video from earlier and sitting back in the chair, a hand in my shorts.

Colton licked his lips and pulled his shorts off, his stiff cock springing free, hitting his belly with a dull thud. His tip glistened with precum as he grabbed himself in a fist, opening his legs and massaging his balls with his other hand.

We jerked off again, but this time, we couldn't keep our hands to ourselves. It was impossible. I had to feel him. Needed to hold him. I *wanted* to be the reason why Colton's eyes rolled back. I reached for him, and he reached for me. Slow and soft, I relished every stroke, my toes curling into the floor as Colton stroked me all the way to an orgasm, cum dribbling out of my tip and over his closed fist. He spilled, too, his cock twitching in my grip, the both of us breathless and spent.

It was in that moment I was hit with a stark realization: this wasn't fake. Nothing about us being together was fake. No matter what rules or regulations or whatever the fuck else we set up between us, my feelings for Colton were *very* real and *very* intense.

And I had to tell him. Tomorrow, I'd talk to him. I'd open up and bare it all for him, show him that I wanted him. That I'd never hurt him again.

But I'd talk to him tomorrow. Tonight had already been far too turbulent. By the time we climbed into bed, the two of us were asleep in minutes, wrapped up in each other's arms, the pillows I had put up between us being tossed to the floor so that nothing separated us.

22

COLTON COOPER

THE CLINKING of dishes in the sink drifted out of the archway leading into the kitchen. Sunlight poured through the open window. I could hear Kendall and Jax whispering together on the couch as I walked past them, a coffee cup in my hand. Neither of them looked at me.

A couple of days had passed since that trashier of a dinner without much happening. Everyone sort of avoided each other, which wasn't necessarily ideal, but it did give time for Eric and me to brainstorm. The brainstorming sessions were usually pretty productive, until one of us would inevitably get hard and end up whipping it out, starting another friendly little stroke session between two fake boyfriends.

There were a couple of moments where it seemed like Eric wanted to talk about something. Maybe it was the post-nut clarity causing him to finally confront those emotions he was hell-bent on running away from. Maybe he was finally ready to say sorry for the shit he'd put me through back when we were *actually* together.

Whatever it was, I wasn't finding out anytime soon. He'd stay quiet, even when I asked him point-blank if there was something he wanted to talk about. He'd shake his head and steer the conversation back to the case, throwing around theories and asking me questions I didn't have any answers to. I allowed the redirection. If Eric didn't want to have a heart-to-heart with me, then I'd just have to keep my walls up.

As if I even have any walls left standing.

I tried to focus on the case. It felt like we were getting close to cracking it. Pieces were beginning to fall into place, but the image was still blurry. We were still missing one huge piece of the puzzle: the will.

Without knowing what was on the will, we weren't sure who stood to gain the most from my mother's death.

Then there was the matter of trying to figure out the timeline of my mom's relationship with Jax. I didn't trust the guy as far as I could throw him, but that didn't mean I suspected him of murder... *unless* he gave me reason to suspect him. If he was still dating my mom around the time of her death, then he would certainly be close enough to kill her without suspicion.

It was a lot to think about.

"Hey, Dad."

I greeted my father as I entered the kitchen. He was washing some dishes, looking relaxed and already in his pajama pants and T-shirt. I'd always been a momma's boy growing up, but that's not to say that the relationship between my dad and me wasn't ever special. There were a couple of years—especially during my early teenage years—when we butted heads more often than not, but it never turned aggressive or out of control. And when he and my mom split, as much of a shock as it was to all of us, it appeared to be an even bigger shock to him. We grew closer after the divorce, which felt slightly ironic to me.

"How ya doing, Colt?" he asked me, setting a mug down on the counter. The window above the sink looked out to the mountains, traced by the light of a slowly setting sun.

"Tired, stressed, slightly hungry. What else is new?"

My dad gave me an emphatic look. He reached out a hand and squeezed my shoulder. He had kind eyes—always did, even when he was angry. I loved my dad, and that made it almost impossible to fathom him being responsible for my mother's death.

"You've got to take it easy. Before you get my crow's feet. I don't think that gene skips a generation."

I huffed out a breath and waved a hand. "Please, I'll be getting Botox way before that happens. Preventative measure."

My dad chuckled. He turned and went back to putting away the dishes. I leaned on the counter, looking out the window. I could see Jen riding her bike through the field of lavender stalks, her bright blue helmet looked like a streaking comet shooting across the ground.

"Mom would have approved of him," my dad said.

"Eric," he clarified off my confused expression. "I had a talk with him this morning. He's a good guy."

I already knew Eric and my dad had spoken after breakfast. Eric gave me a rundown on everything they'd talked about. Eric tried to pry as hard as he could, digging for information without pushing too hard. He didn't get anything, or so we thought.

It looked like he did get something: my dad's admiration.

"Yeah," I said, "he is."

"You know, it makes me really proud to see you this happy. Really proud."

"Dad, you don't have to get all sentimental."

"I know, I know. I just—life's been, well, it's been insane, to put it lightly. I sometimes wake up and expect everything to snap back to the way it was. Back to when you were ten years old, riding a bike with your sisters, getting teased by your brothers, bringing home straight As, and asking for ice cream for dinner. Everything was so simple, and then all of a sudden, it wasn't."

I gave a slow nod, sucked in a breath. "That's just the way life goes, Dad. Things are simple one minute and completely fucked-up the next. That's why I try to just soak in all the good times, all the quiet times. You taught me that."

My father was always one for taking a moment to reflect. He would make us all gather around for a couple of minutes before the start of every vacation, and we would just hug each other and be happy for the times ahead. It was a good way of kicking things off and always set the tone. It didn't stop my family from falling apart, but it gave me moments encased in amber I could always look back fondly on.

"Colt, now that I've got you here, I think I should tell you…" My dad trailed off. He looked down at his feet, his hands clenched in tight fists. What the hell had him so anxious?

"What is it?" I asked, cocking my head.

"I don't even know how—it's complicated. I just don't want you to think any different of me. I don't want you to hate me."

I reeled back with surprise. "Hate you? For what, Dad? I can't ever hate you."

"For hurting you. For hurting your mom. For hiding the truth from all of you for all this time."

My eyebrows nearly fell off my forehead. I was not expecting all this when I had come over to the kitchen to grab a beer. My father looked like he was on the brink of tears. He'd always been a bit of a crier, but this felt different, like he was struggling with something heavy and painful. Something that gnawed at him from the inside. He put a hand on the back of his neck.

"Hiding what?" I asked, growing worried.

"Hiding my—"

"What's dad crying about now?" Kendall's voice was like nails on a chalkboard. They grated at my nerves, making the hair on my arms stand straight. I had always had a difficult time connecting with Kendall, and this trip wasn't making that any easier by any means.

My dad instantly retreated back into his shell. His

back straightened, and his bottom lip stiffened. He turned and closed the cupboard door with a bit of a slam. "Nothing," he said as Jackson entered the kitchen. He held an empty wine bottle in his hand, wearing a T-shirt from one of Dolly Parton's concerts. That used to be my mom's favorite artist.

Just a coincidence, I'm sure.

The mood in the kitchen instantly shifted. As if an invisible force swept in and made the air ten degrees colder and twenty pounds heavier. "Kendall, you can be a little bit softer with your words, you know."

"Don't therapize me, Colton. I don't have to be soft with anything. Words, life, *men*." She put a hand on Jackson's shoulder and hung off him like a monkey about to climb up a tree.

I rolled my eyes. My sister was older than me but acted as if she was fifteen years younger. Her maturity levels were lacking, which probably explained why she and my mom never got along.

Kendall lighting my mom's house on fire likely didn't help their relationship.

"If we interrupted anything, I'm sorry." Jackson's apology caught me by surprise, and judging by my father's cracked jaw, it caught him by surprise, too. Kendall even looked up at Jackson with a face that said he'd need to do some explaining later.

"It was nothing, it's fine," my dad said. He cleared his throat and clapped his hands together. The warm smile and kind eyes slowly appeared back in their proper places. "I'm going to bed, but let's try and have a good day tomorrow, alright? We've got the field day set up. That should be fun, huh? And then we've got a murder-mystery dinner planned. So let's just let go of everything that happened and try to honor Amelia's memory the best we can." My dad gave me and my sister a pointed look. "Okay?"

We nodded in unison, like we were back to being little kids promising to be on our best behavior. He left the kitchen, taking whatever confession he was about to make with him. I knew I had to go talk to Eric about this. He'd be the only one I could vent to, the only one who could make this all make sense. I had to go find him.

And maybe we could even fool around for a little before. Just to clear my head, of course.

"Where the hell are you going?" Kendall asked as I grabbed a beer from the fridge. "Sorry, were those words too harsh for you?"

"No, the only thing that's harsh here is the charcoal eyeshadow you thought was a good idea to slather around your eyes. Looks like you went chimney diving."

I turned on my heel and left my sister speechless. Don't come after a gay sibling if you aren't ready to get read. Sorry. I didn't make the rules.

Just followed them.

23

ERIC RUIZ

"OH, you should have seen her face," Colton said, laughing. "She was shocked. Served her right—that eyeshadow really was a crime against humanity."

We were in the yard, walking down the cobblestone path that led out past the tall wooden fence that surrounded the property, opening onto a trail that traced its way around the deep purple fields of sweet smelling lavender surrounding the property. Colton had been explaining what had happened in the kitchen, ending it with the burn he'd left on his sister.

"Was your dad okay?" I asked.

"I'm not sure," he answered, his voice trailing off. I heard some worry in his tone, some anxiety. I couldn't imagine how unmoored he felt, having to come back to one of his mother's favorite places without her while dealing with some turbulent family dynamics. It was painful to watch. I wanted to do all I could to protect him, to wrap him up in my arms and keep him safe from all the bullshit the world wanted to throw his way.

The night was a quiet one. I looked up at the star-filled sky, wondering how the hell my life had landed me here. A serene sense of calm and peace filled me as I looked to my left, Colton walking alongside me, his knuckles grazing mine as our hands gravitated toward each other. Like two magnets constantly getting pulled together.

I reached for his hand. He didn't pull away. His fingers locked with mine, causing my heart to swell as heat spiraled up my palm, swirling around my wrist and forearm, spreading through me like an out-of-control forest fire.

Being here with Colton, walking under a blanket of stars, listening to the crunch of rocks under our feet and the chirp of crickets in the air... it felt... it felt *right*. It felt good. It felt *real*.

"What do you think my dad was going to tell me?"

His question landed like a shooting star, sparking a dozen different theories, none of them more valid than the last. "I don't know," I answered honestly. "You know your dad better than I do."

Although I did have a good idea of who William was from my preliminary research. He had a large online footprint, which made it easy to see his entire eighteen-year-long work history and social media presence. I saw big dates marked with a flurry of photos (weddings, birthdays, graduations), while the darker dates were absent or appeared as blips in his timeline:

Amelia and William have separated.

A quick status update mentioning the passing of his father.

Another status update about his stepping down from the board of his company.

But what I noticed about those moments was that he always seemed to turn it around. In days, he'd be back to posting smiling photos in the Bahamas or traveling through Europe or surrounded by his kids at another birthday party. He didn't seem to let the world beat him down, which was why I was surprised to see him shuffling his feet around the villa this morning, his shoulders slumped and head bowed.

He resembled a man that had been thrown in the ring and come out bloodied and bruised, every bone hurting with each tiny movement.

"I don't know him, that's the thing." Colton let out an exasperated breath. A breeze stirred the tall stalks of light purple lavender. They were planted at the villa in honor of Amelia, who had loved the flowers. Just like my mom had. "He's been pretty distant with me for a while now. I go to his birthday parties and see him around the holidays, but we haven't actually spent quality time together in years. And it got even worse after my mom's death. That's why him acting like that in the kitchen surprised the fuck out of me."

"It has to be something big," I said. "Maybe he knew your mom had been with Jax all those years?"

Colton winced, shook his head.

"Or maybe," I continued theorizing, "maybe he wants

to tell you he's been seeing someone? Maybe he found another woman and feels bad even bringing her up."

"Hmm, maybe..." Colton's hand squeezed mine. I could see the gears spinning in his head, his bright blue eyes catching some of the moonlight and reflecting it back at me like a pair of perfectly cut diamonds.

"How's things with your dad been?" Colton asked. We had stopped walking, the villa behind us and the mountains ahead, rolling fields made up of dark purple waves in between. "I remember it being a little rocky back when we were in the academy."

I leaned against a fence post, Colton's hand slipping from mine. My memories were dragged right back to those "rocky" days, when my dad and I were simply butting heads and not locked in a full-on nuclear war together. "Things haven't gotten any better."

"Oh? Weren't you two really close?"

"We were. Especially after my mom passed. I was just twelve, but I barely ever left his side after that," I said, a little piece of me warming at the realization that Colton remembered all these things about me. He remembered the fabric that made up the threads of my past without needing to be told or filled in. He just knew, the same way I knew about him.

"What happened?" Colton asked. I realized I had been walling myself off. Thinking of my dad—it was painful.

Speaking about him? That shit was torture.

"We stopped talking. He's basically dead to me."

"Damn, that bad?"

"That bad." I didn't want to talk about this. I didn't want to soil such a perfect night with such rotten thoughts. But Colton wasn't taking my silence as an answer. He prodded some more, asking me about the details, not knowing the details had to do with him.

"He found some texts. Between you and I. He was using my phone to order some food, and he tapped the wrong app. When he read what we had written to each other, he flipped. Threw my phone across the room, wanted me out of his house. He told me to come back after I 'fixed' myself.

"That was the night I ended things with you. I got back to our dorm, and I remember it being the nastiest fucking storm outside, and you were sitting on the couch, excited I got back. You already had the controllers out and the video game playing on the TV."

"You were dripping wet. I could tell something was wrong right off the bat." Colton's eyes drilled through mine. "I had no idea that's what happened, though..."

"I was pissed. Furious. But I didn't know at who. I didn't realize I was just pissed off at myself. So I dug my heels in and ended it with you in the quickest and nastiest way I could think of. I said some fucked-up shit to you that night, and nothing I say now can erase those words, but Colt, you have to believe me when I say I regret them with every single fucking cell in my body." I grabbed both his hands in mine. Tears were sliding down my cheek. I couldn't stop them, didn't try. My lip trembled as the welled-up emotion pushed through my throat, blocking me from speaking for a second.

I swallowed, cleared my throat. Colton's blue eyes were like calm pools of ocean water, calming me down. There were tears collecting at the corners of those blue pools.

"I'm sorry," I said. "I should have never said I'd never you love, that I'd never be with you. It was a lie. I was scared. I was lost. I was hurt and acting out of pure fear. I'm so sorry, Colt. So fucking sorry."

The tears were coming down harder, my cheeks wet and my heart hammering. I rubbed at my face with my knuckles, my hand shaking. I didn't know what would come from this confession, but I knew I couldn't stop it. The train had derailed, and it was barreling off the tracks.

"I loved you, Colton. I still do. I've always loved you. You make me happy in ways I've never been able to find again ever since I pushed you away. Being around you in simple silence can be the highlight of my day, and that doesn't happen with anyone else. You're my one, Colton. I pushed you away because I was in denial, because the men around me were the most toxic kind, and all I wanted was their approval.

"But not anymore. I don't give a fuck about those backwards-ass cavemen. I'm an out and proud gay man, and I'm staring into the eyes of the man of my dreams."

Colton blinked through the shock.

"Eric, that night... it was really rough for me. I—I was head over heels for you, man. And you crushed me. I was in a really bad mental state after that."

Colton's words felt like a visceral stab through the chest. I could almost pinpoint the exact muscles and cartilage that were torn apart. I never wanted to hurt him, *never*. In my fucked-up mental state, I had justified it as giving Colton his freedom back. He deserved to be with someone who wasn't ashamed of holding his hand. He deserved the world, and I had felt like a piece of dog shit stuck to someone's sneaker.

"I'm so sorry," I repeated, finding it hard to even speak. I'd only felt this kind of constricting emotion once before—at my mother's funeral. Never since, not until now. "I should have leaned into you instead of away from you. I see that now, and I hate that young Eric couldn't see that then. I pushed you away, thinking that was the answer, but the answer was staring me in the face the entire time. I don't want to make that same mistake again, Colt. I don't want to ever let you go.

"Please, let's stop with this fake charade between us. Let's go back to how we used to be, but better. I want to be with you, Colton. I want you to be my *real* boyfriend."

His big lips curled into a smile. His hands found mine, his body moving closer to mine. I could feel his breath tickling my chin as he looked into my eyes, inches separating us, starlight bathing us. I was scared I had gone too far, opened up too much. I was scared I would push him away again, but this time for a different reason.

His smile made all those fears disappear. Vanished, like the weight I had strapped to my shoulders. Colton pushed in for a kiss, his smile transferring to my lips, our tongues dancing and our bodies melting together.

It was the perfect moment. It would have stayed

perfect, too, if it weren't for the ear-splitting screech that made us both turn around toward the villa.

"Someone help!"

"That's Jen." Without even looking at me, Colton started to run to the villa with me close behind.

24

ERIC RUIZ

WE DIDN'T WASTE A SECOND. Colton recognized his sister's terrified screech; it was clear she needed help. We had no idea from what, but that didn't slow us down. It only did the opposite, making us run faster through the yard, dashing around the pool and launching through the doors leading into the kitchen. Colton's dad was running down the hall, Archie close behind him.

"What? What happened?" William asked as we all turned the corner into the living room, where Jen stood like a statue, her arm outstretched and pointing toward something dark in the corner of the room.

"*That* happened!" She took a couple of shaky steps backward, her entire body giving a repulsed shake. "I was just about to curl up on the couch and read my book when I see that thing moving in the corner of my eye."

I took a couple of steps closer and realized what I was looking at: a tarantula. A big one, hairy and aiming all its hundred little eyes in our direction, its front legs up and its fangs bared in a warning to all of us.

Don't get close, or I'll fuck you up.

I lurched back, nearly falling over the coffee table. "Oh hell no," I said. "*Nombre no.* I do not do spiders. No way."

I was so scared that my Spanish was slipping out. Colton chuckled and stepped forward. He grabbed a large clear vase off the table, taking the roses out and placing them gently on the ground. "Anyone have a thick piece of paper?"

The tarantula didn't move. Matthew and Krystine came running in at that moment, looking like they had just been about to get in bed, wearing matching silk pajamas. "Everything al—holy shit," Matt said when he realized what we were all staring at. "That's one big fucking spider."

Krystine shrieked and bolted in the opposite direction. Colton spotted a magazine and grabbed it, ripping off the cover so he had one solid and thick piece of paper with him as he crossed the room.

"Be careful with the vase," I said to him as he got closer. "Don't break it in your hand."

Part of my intense fear subsided as I grew worried for Colt, even though he looked like he was in complete control of the situation. He moved slowly, tiptoeing toward the intruder. Wendy made a sound as she clutched her arms tight around her chest, Archie at her side. He had a large knife in his hand.

When the hell did he get that?

"Just let me handle it," Archie said, taking a step forward.

Colton put a hand back while still facing the tarantula. "I've got it, don't worry."

"Babe," Wendy said, looking down at the knife. "You'd need a flamethrower if you wanted to kill it."

Colton inched forward. If he was scared, then he was doing a great job of hiding it. I felt bad sticking back while Colton forged ahead to face the danger, but arachnophobia was a bitch—especially when the subject of that arachnophobia was a nasty-looking spider that was nearly the size of a small house cat. I'd taken down gangsters and mobsters and stalkers, but facing a tarantula was where I drew the line.

Thankfully, Colton didn't seem to have the same issue. He raised the vase over the spider, which pivoted so that its raised legs and fangs were aimed directly at Colton. I held my breath. Logically, I knew that there'd be no *actual* danger to Colton unless he was deathly allergic to tarantula venom, but logic didn't stop my heart from racing and my palms from sweating.

Colton moved like swift lightning, dropping the vase over the spider, the rim of it clicking against the floor as he trapped the hairy monster inside. Everyone in the room let out a collective sigh of relief, which quickly turned into a collective gasp as Colton nearly let the tarantula loose as he tried to squeeze the paper underneath the vase.

He maintained control and trapped the spider inside the vase, rising back up to his feet and holding it in the air like a trophy. "See, that wasn't that bad," he said, smiling.

I couldn't even look in his direction. "Okay, okay, go throw it outside. Preferably outside of the property line."

Archie ran ahead of Colton so he could open the door for him, the butcher knife still in his hand. Colton went out into the yard and released his new friend, where I hoped he'd promptly be eaten by a hawk or falcon or whatever other natural predator that terrifying creature might have.

"You okay?" Colton asked me as he came back into the living room. "You look a little pale."

"I'm fine, I'm fine," I said, just now realizing how light-headed I felt.

Jen rose up from the couch and took her brother into a tight hug. "Thank you for always saving the day, Colt." She grabbed the book she'd been planning to read and started toward the arching doorway. "And with that, I'm out. I need to go lay down after that."

The rest of the group started to disperse. It was already late, and frankly, Jen's idea didn't sound all that bad. I wouldn't mind spending some time with Colton in bed, especially now that we didn't have to worry about kissing limits or pillow borders.

"Ready to hit the hay?" I asked, grabbing Colton's hand in mine. "You must be exhausted after rescuing us all from being held hostage."

Colton cocked his head, smiled at me. I saw a mixture of the old Colton and the present Colton staring at me. Was that what made second chances like ours so special?

I could see his past and could now envision his future with me, all wrapped up together in a sparkling bow. "I kind of want to walk around a bit, actually. I'm a little too hyped up right now."

"Let's explore, then. There's still an entire section of this villa I haven't seen yet." I squeezed Colton's hand in mine. His grin was wide, dimples making tiny craters in his cheeks. I couldn't stop myself from leaning in and stealing a kiss. His smile only grew wider against my lips, his hand resting on my chest, right above my heart.

Good. He'll feel the beats that are for him.

We separated when a cough from the doorway startled us. I turned to see Colton's grandmother, Macy, wearing black-and-white polka-dotted pajama pants and a Lady Gaga T-shirt. She had two bowls of ice cream in her hands, her thin eyebrow arched as she looked at us. "Sorry, boys, didn't want to ruin the moment. I just was wondering if you two knew what all that commotion was about earlier? Luna and I were outside."

"Oh, Jen spotted a huge tarantula, so I came and relocated it." Colton's cheeks had a rosy pink blush to them, likely from being caught by his grandma with his tongue down my throat.

"A tarantula? Oh, don't tell Luna, then. She'll be on the first flight back home." She shook her head and looked around the room. "Where exactly did you relocate it, Colt?"

"I could only get it past your guys' bedroom door before I had to let it free."

"Colton Richard Martin Conners, don't even joke around like that."

Colton and I both started to chuckle, Macy joining in the laughter before shuffling away in her slippers, calling a "good night, bastards" over her shoulder.

I looked back to Colton. "I didn't know you had middle names."

"I don't," he said, starting down the hallway that wound around the kitchen. "My grandmother just loves throwing random names in whenever we would get in trouble with her."

"Gotcha," I said, laughing some more. My eyes dropped down to Colton's juicy butt as he led the way down the brightly lit hallway. I tried not to be fixated by his apple bottom, but it was hard—pun fully intended. Especially now that we were officially official. I wanted to grab his hips and pull him back onto me, kissing his neck and pressing him up against the wall so he could feel just how excited I was at being official.

"Have you checked out the library?" Colton asked over his shoulder. I dragged my gaze back up to his.

"No, I haven't yet."

"Oh, you'll love it. Come, it's this way." Colton continued through the villa. We passed a couple of bedrooms, one of them with loud hip-hop music coming from under the threshold. There was a study and two offices, along with a spa-like bathroom that I made a mental note of to come back to. I had to give that rainfall steam shower a try.

We took a right through a set of wide double doors

and stepped into the library, entering a book lover's paradise with a giddy feeling in my gut. Maybe it was the residual adrenaline working its way through my system after that tarantula encounter, or maybe it was just the simple fact of being here with Colton—my boyfriend. I could hardly even believe that was a real thought. That we were actually a *real* couple. It felt so freeing, being able to express myself to Colton and having those emotions reciprocated right back.

Why hadn't I done this sooner?

The library room was massive, with six long bookshelves placed strategically throughout the circular space that gave the illusion of being surrounded by a never-ending collection of books. The walls were covered in a rich green wallpaper with flowers printed throughout, stretching all the way up to the domed ceiling. There was a nook with the comfiest-looking maroon couch I'd ever seen, an antique floor lamp set behind it, a window above it. Colton went and opened it, allowing a gentle breeze to drift into the space.

I immediately got lost looking through the different spines, seeing the different kinds of books that had made this library their permanent home. I saw a few genealogy books, some history books, a couple of thrillers, and an entire section of spicy romance. There was another shelf dedicated to the sciences and another shelf that appeared to hold just the classics, bound in sturdy leather. Colton came up behind me, wrapping his arms around my waist and resting his head against my shoulders.

"Mmm, you smell good," he said.

"So do you." I tried not to think of how much nicer this would feel with all our clothes off.

"See anything you want to check out of the library?"

"There's a couple."

Colton kissed the back of my neck. It sent a flurry of butterfly-shaped fireworks sparkling through my chest. I rolled my head back, shutting my eyes as Colton's grip around me tightened.

"I used to spend a lot of time here as a kid. But mostly playing on my Game Boy. Archie would take it from me sometimes, but he'd never come to the library, so I started to come here just to play."

"Archie's a little bit of a dick, huh?"

Colton huffed. "He's gotten better, but yeah. We've had our issues."

He planted another kiss on my neck. I never realized just how good lips back there could feel. "When did he get into the drugs and gambling?" I asked, wanting to paint a clear timeline but getting my thoughts scrambled as Colton's hands shifted lower.

"Around the time of my parents' divorce, right? Took him three to get back on his feet. Now he's got that tech company with Wendy and seems to be doing great."

"When did Wendy come into the picture?"

Colton's lips grazed my skin again. He spoke against me, the vibrations of his voice rocking through me. "I don't really know. I think they met in rehab, actually."

"Hmm, interesting," I said, even though I couldn't focus on anything Colton was telling me now that I could feel him getting hard against me. I turned around, keeping his arms around me. He looked up into my eyes, his blue orbs swirling with a kind of magic I didn't think I'd ever grow tired of. The spell was cast; I was his now.

"You're so fucking handsome," I said, tracing the lines of his jaw with my thumb. His cock twitched against mine, both of us not being shy about how turned on we were. I licked my lips, entranced by this beautiful man. He was all sharp angles and soft lips and bright eyes, his hard cock pushing against my thigh as he leaned in and kissed me again. I released a moan, the sound rising from my chest and being swallowed by Colt. His hands dropped to my ass. He squeezed, and I gave him another moan, our lips locked and our bodies fitting together.

I wanted to meld with him, become one with him. I needed him to ride me, needed to feel myself buried deep inside him. I needed—

A sound made us jerk backward. It was a voice. Macy again? No, it sounded younger, and the person was just outside the window, speaking in whispers. Colton looked at me and mouthed, "Who is that?"

I shrugged. All I wanted was to get Colton to the bedroom, where I planned on tearing off his clothes and worshipping every inch of his body until the sun came up. I grabbed his hand and was about to pull him out of the room when something else caught my attention. Whoever was whispering wasn't speaking English.

It sounded Italian... but who here spoke Italian, and why now?

Instead of tugging Colton toward the exit, I put a finger to my lip and tiptoed toward the window instead.

25

COLTON COOPER

"Sì, sono qui, Lito. No, non abbiamo ancora letto il testamento."

I cocked my head as Eric and I crouched together by the window. I mouthed out "Wendy," surprised at her fluency in Italian. I didn't know all that much about my brother's wife, but this fact surprised me.

"Okay, okay. Ti chiamo domani. Bye, ti amo."

Wendy hung up the call, the sound of her footsteps tapping against the concrete growing more and more distant.

I looked down, realizing Eric had been recording the conversation. I could have kissed him. In fact, I decided I *should* kiss him. I leaned in, pressing my lips against his, my hand falling on his knee so that I didn't tip over.

"What's that for?" Eric said, smiling as we both stood back up.

"For being my boyfriend."

His smile widened, matching mine. It sounded good:

boyfriend. I didn't think it'd be something I'd be calling Eric, not when I first bumped into him in that coffee shop, my walls still high and seemingly impenetrable after my last shitty relationships. I should have known Eric would have no trouble barreling right through my defenses. This "fake" situation we had set up was never really fake, and I could see that now. The butterflies that fluttered to life every time he was around was impossible to fake. We had too much shared history between us, too many warm memories, the kind that out shadowed the shittier moments.

And he apologized. It was all I ever really needed from him. An acknowledgment of the pain he'd caused me and a reasoning behind it. I had known him and his dad had been incredibly close, so I always assumed he might have had something to do with how Eric pushed me away, but hearing the entire story erased any residual hurt I was still holding on to from that lightning-filled night.

"So what do you think Wendy was saying?" I asked as we moved away from the window, walking through an aisle of tome-like books, golden letters scrawled down their spines.

"I'm not entirely sure, but Yvette is fluent in Italian. I'm sending her the recording now."

I looked at my watch. A little past midnight, which meant she'd still likely be awake with the time difference.

"Does Archie speak Italian?" Eric asked.

"Not that I know of, unless he picked it up recently. Who could Wendy have been talking to?"

"Maybe a relative? Did she ever say she was from Italy?"

I tried to scrub through every conversation I'd had with Archie and Wendy, but I couldn't remember if Wendy's nationality had ever come up. She always just seemed like a blank slate to me. Someone who clearly had a good effect on my brother, which was really all that mattered to me. If he was happy and healthy and it was because of her, then all the more power to her.

"I don't know," I answered, pursing my lips.

"That's fine. I'm sure it's no big deal." Eric put his hand on my arm, his thumb rubbing a soft circle on my elbow. "Alright, ready to get to bed?"

"Yes," I said, pushing in for another kiss. "But I'm not planning on sleeping if that's what you're thinking."

"That's totally fine with me," he said against my lips, his hands moving to my hips as he held me close to him. I put my head on his chest, feeling completely at home in Eric's arms. It didn't matter that I was in an entirely different country, surrounded by chaos and turmoil and pissed-off tarantulas; it still felt like home as long as Eric was there with me. It was a kind of special skill only Eric possessed. Like he held the antidote to all my worries and problems just by being there with me.

I kissed his neck, his grip tightening. I felt him twitch between us, my cock responding by doing the same. I licked his neck, my hands going under his shirt. I couldn't resist touching him. His soft chest hair brushed against my palm as I ran my hands over his nipples, my tongue tracing the line of his jaw.

I managed to pry myself off him before we got too carried away. I tucked my erection into the waistband of my pants so that I wasn't walking around with a full-on tent pitched in my crotch. Eric licked his lips, his fingers slipping through mine as we hurried to the bedroom, both of us giddy and horny and so fucking *happy*.

Our clothes were off the second the door shut behind us. I pressed myself against Eric and kissed him as we stumbled backward, falling onto the bed in a tangle of limbs and cock. I rutted my hips, feeling him push back. A delicious pressure built up in my balls as I rubbed myself against him. "God, you feel so fucking good, Eric."

I ran my hands up and down his body. He was lying down, his legs open so that I could fit between them. He was the definition of a beefy bear, hairy and curvy and so, so fucking sexy.

He made his thick cock twitch as I held him in my hand. I slowly stroked him, up and down and up and down, appreciating every single inch. All seven and a half of them. He rubbed his nipples as I spat in my hand, slicking him up. He groaned with pleasure as I jerked him off, using both hands. I started to buck up into my fist, precum leaking from the tip of his cock. I took that as an opportunity to lean in and get a taste.

"Ooooh, fuck," he hissed out as I took him in my mouth. He opened his legs a little wider and threaded his hands through my hair. I let him control me, pushing my head down so that I swallowed more and more of his stiff length. "That's it, Colt. Suck it just like that. Good boy."

Every nerve cell in my body instantaneously

combusted. Flames shot through me, my cock pulsing. I stuffed him down my throat, his scent filling me as I breathed him in, working my tongue around the head of his cock. I wasn't scared to get messy or loud, saliva dripping down his balls as I gagged around his size.

"Swallow it, baby. Fuck yeah. You look so fucking sexy with my cock in your mouth."

I looked up at him, smiling around his dick. The salty-sweet flavor of his precum exploded around my taste buds. I wanted more, so much more. My hole twitched, my entire body crying out for him. I reached back and touched myself, my fingers already wet, slipping in without any resistance.

"God, Eric, you taste so good. I can't get enough of you."

His smolder nearly made me come right then and there. He grabbed his cock and pressed it against my cheek, slapping me with it. I grinned, rubbing my face in the crook of his thigh, burying my nose just next to his balls. I licked at the sensitive skin, my finger probing into my ass, getting myself ready for the main event.

"I need you to fuck me, Eric. Please. Fuck me. Make me yours."

His eyes lit up like two bright stars fallen straight from the night sky.

"Get up here," he said, pulling me up onto him so that his lips locked around mine. His hands roamed my body, grabbing my ass and spreading me open. I felt the cool breeze from the fan whirling above us, but I still had sweat beading on my forehead from the heat that blazed inside me.

We kissed in a way that completely unraveled me. It made everything that happened tonight all the more real and yet still made it seem like a dream.

Eric and I, together, officially. No more rules or boundaries, just us, being as raw and vulnerable with each other as we possibly could.

I reached back and lined his cock up with my hole, my entrance still wet from my finger. I sat back, feeling him push inside me. My eyes opened wide as my jaw slowly dropped, my lips forming an O. Eric looked up at me with hunger in his gaze. His fingers dug into my hips as he guided me down.

"Whoa, whoa," I said, feeling a sting. "Grab the lube. You're way too big," I said, already breathless but feral for Eric's cock. I had to have him inside me; I just needed a little help with getting him there.

He leaned over and reached for the drawer in the nightstand, the head of his cock still pushing into me. I moaned, the sting lessening as my body relaxed, accepting him in. He popped open the cap on the lube bottle and squirted some into his hand. He reached for my cock first and gave me a few eyes-rolling-to-the-back-of-my-head strokes before he pulled himself out and spread the lube on his dick. He set the bottle back on the nightstand and locked eyes with me, his hands coming back to my hips.

"Ready, baby?"

I nodded, biting my bottom lip as I sat back. This

time, his cock slid in much easier, the pain no longer there. Instead, an overwhelming bliss followed the sensation of being filled by Eric's thick cock. He gave one thrust and buried himself balls-deep, drawing a shout of pleasure directly from my chest. I fell forward, gripping his chest as I arched my back and took him in, his thrusts pushing him deeper and deeper. Skin slapped against skin; moans mixed with grunts mixed with cries mixed with words I wasn't even sure were real. Eric had me speaking in tongues, his rhythmic thrusts hitting me in all the right places.

"Shit, Colt, you've already got me so close."

"Me too," I said, looking down at my tightening balls and leaking, bouncing cock. A string of clear precum connected me with Eric, his dark happy trail sticky and wet. I rubbed his chest, riding him like I was some sort of cowboy on top of a bucking bronco.

"That's it, that's it, oh fuck, baby, I'm gonna come."

"Do it, Eric. Fill me up with your load. *Fuuuuck.*"

Eric gave one final thrust and buried himself to the hilt, his head falling back and his throat flushing pink. No words formed, only a guttural and animalistic moan that told me he was giving me exactly what I wanted.

It pushed me over the edge with him. I shot ropes of cum, some of it going past Eric and hitting the headboard. My entire body gave a spasm as the orgasm tore through me, my hole quivering around Eric's still-swollen cock, taking all I could from him as I gave him all I had.

After what felt like an eternity of pleasure, I was able

to put together a couple of cohesive sentences. "That was mind-blowingly good, holy shit."

Eric, still inside me, kissed me, his fingers tracing lazy shapes on my lower back. "I think I can actually go for round two already."

"Really?" I asked, noting that my own erection still hadn't gone anywhere. I gave my hips a playful swirl. "We won't need more lube, not with your cum dripping out of me."

Eric shook his head, grinning. "You're so fucking bad. I love it." He gave a thrust, and just like that, round two was on.

We went all the way up to round four before our bodies gave in, sleep overcoming us, the sex continuing on into my dreams, leaving me waking up the next morning with a smile on and my heart (and hole) full.

ERIC RUIZ

I SLEPT LIKE A BABY, with Colton curled up in my arms, his gentle breaths working like white noise and lulling me right to sleep. It had been the perfect way to end a perfect night. I woke up scared it had all just been a wispy dream, floating off into the sky the second my eyelashes fluttered open, but Colton's warm body tucked against mine reassured me that it was all, in fact, very real.

I kissed the back of his head and stretched out underneath the covers. Sunlight was already slipping in through the drawn curtains, creating a peaceful orange-and-blue glow that made the room appear as if under an Instagram filter. My phone was on the nightstand set on "do not disturb." I turned the setting off and was greeted with a couple of emails I promptly ignored, tapping instead on Yvette's text bubble.

She's telling someone named Lito that they haven't

read the will yet. She says she'll call him tomorrow and that she loves him. Does that help?

Yup, that's exactly what I needed. Thank you!

I put the phone back on the nightstand. Yvette's translation certainly helped, but it also brought up about a thousand different questions. Who the hell was Lito? Why was Wendy so concerned about the will? And why was she ending the call with an "I love you"? It didn't make much sense, not until I figured out who the hell was on the other end of that call.

Colton stirred awake, rolling over so he faced me. He threw one leg over me, rubbing his morning wood against my thigh. I closed my eyes and smiled. Was this what romance movies always tried to show? The warm-gooey-over-the-moon feeling that swelled through me as Colton cuddled into me, his warm breath tickling my neck, his hand resting just above my heart.

With his eyes still shut, he gave me a groggy "Morning, stud" before kissing my cheek.

My cock twitched under the comforter, making the heavy white fabric bounce. The questions about Wendy were slowly getting pushed to the background as Colton's stiff cock moved directly to the foreground.

"Did Yvette text you?" Colton asked, sounding slightly more awake. The questions fell back into focus. I nodded and told him what Yvette had translated.

"Love?" Colton repeated as he sat up, fully awake now. "And who the hell is Lito?"

"My thoughts exactly," I said, looking up at a confused Colton. The comforter was still bunched up around my twitching length. I tried ignoring it for now. "And why is she talking to Lito about the will?"

"Which she might not even be on."

"Huh?"

Colton covered his mouth as he yawned before explaining. "My mom never liked her. Archie and my mom had some intense arguments over that, which probably only made my mom dislike her even more."

"But your mom wouldn't leave Archie off the will, would she?"

He shook his head. "Nah, I doubt that. Even with all the drama, Archie was still my mom's favorite. She'd never say, but it was kind of obvious."

This was all adding up to something; I just wasn't entirely sure I had the math down just yet. Something was off. I needed to figure out who this Lito guy was and why Wendy seemed to be so invested in the will, reporting to him in a language no one even knew she spoke.

It would take some poking around where I didn't belong to figure things out. We had our field day later, which could provide some opportunity to dig for information while everyone was distracted with some friendly competition. I glanced at the clock on the nightstand and saw we had a good hour before the chef would have breakfast ready. I still wasn't entirely used to being around so much money, but I also wasn't complaining about the perks.

I sat up and kissed Colton, my hand cupping his face. "We'll figure it out," I said, sliding my hand under the comforter and finding his still-rock-hard morning wood. "But first, let's handle some other business."

We nearly missed breakfast that morning, losing track of time once the comforter was thrown off and warm lips were wrapped around stiff cocks. I could have spent all day sixty-nineing with Colton, but unfortunately, we weren't here on a solo vacation.

Plus, I had work to do.

———

EVERYONE WAS GATHERED outside in loose groups, wearing their sportiest gear and warming up with some jumping jacks and stretches. It was nice to see the family together and friendly with each other, even though there was still an underlying current of tension between Archie, Jackson, and William that sparked up every time one would look at the other. I noticed there was a particularly strong sense of animosity and discomfort coming from William in the way he always appeared to have his back turned toward Jackson, ignoring him even when Kendall called him over to ask a question. Colton's dad would just not look in Jackson's direction.

But William wasn't who I had my focus on this morning. There were two others at this family gathering who had my full attention: Archie and Wendy.

They were sitting on the swinging bench that looked out to the field, just behind the shimmering pool. Archie had his laptop on his lap and an arm thrown over Wendy. They wore matching outfits: dark blue Lululemon pants and tank tops. I was surprised to see so much definition in Archie's arms. He had always come off as lanky and thinly built, but he clearly spent a decent amount of time at the gym. Wendy also looked like she took care of her body, her toned midriff showing a glittering belly button ring as she stood up to join the group. Her hair was tied up in a messy bun, her lighter blonde roots showing against the darker brunette hair dye she had used.

Maybe Lito is their personal trainer?

Colton came up to my side, handing me a bottle of chilled water. I uncapped it and took a swig, handing it back to Colton with a thanks. He looked sexy in a black and blue basketball jersey and oversized black shorts. I would have preferred a shorter inseam if I were being honest, but that was purely for selfish purposes only. He had a thin golden chain that caught the sun as he looked up at me, smiling, bright white teeth showing with that tiny gap in the bottom row.

God damn it, this man was perfect. In every single way. How did I ever find it in me to push him away? What kind of monster had I been? I was a different Eric back then, and I was determined to prove that. I grabbed Colton's hand and pulled him in for a kiss, not caring that we were in public.

He gave me a wink as we separated, his lips shining from the kiss. I was reminded of how he looked with those lips wrapped around my—

"Are you lovebirds ready to get destroyed in flag football?" Jen asked, nudging her brother with an elbow. She wore a bright pink shirt with red shorts and a maroon sweatband around her forehead, holding back most of her freshly washed hair. I could still smell the strawberry-and-mint shampoo she'd used.

"Jen, the last time we played this, my team won against yours by twenty points."

"Which is why you're going to be on my team today," she said, grabbing Colton by the elbow and pulling him away to where her dad, Krystine, and Macy stood. On the other side were Luna and Matt. Jackson and Kendall joined the team I was headed for, while Archie and Wendy got up from the couch and went to Colton's side. They had set up music to play through the Bluetooth speakers, but it cut out just as they were putting on their flag belts.

"Don't worry, I got it," I said, throwing a hand in the air and lightly jogging toward the computer. Archie turned back to help Wendy since she was struggling with the clip on the flag belt.

Perfect. I've got three minutes, tops.

I sat down on the couch and leaned forward, Archie's laptop open to his Spotify page.

I closed out of that and went straight for the web browser.

A lot could be deduced by digging through someone's emails. It was the digital version of rummaging through a person's trash can. Subscriptions to various magazines and newsletters could easily paint a picture about a person's likes and interests, but a couple of emails advertising deals at Nordstrom was barely scratching the surface. There were always other nuggets of gold hiding amongst the spam emails and fishy requests for your credit card info.

And so I went straight to the most popular email provider on the planet and was lucky enough to find Archie logged in. From the screen name at the top, I could tell it was his business account: AC Tech and Security. Immediately, my eyes were drawn to an already read message toward the bottom of the page.

THIS IS OUR FINAL ATTEMPT AT COLLECTING FUNDS BEFORE LEGAL ACTION IS TAKEN.

I clicked it, seeing a message from a loan provider trying to collect—holy shit. They were coming after Archie for two hundred and fifty thousand dollars. So Archie was underwater by a heart-stopping amount, which added up to quite a motive for murder. But taking his own mother's life? That seemed far too extreme for even me to believe, and I'd seen some pretty fucked-up shit in the last six years of my work as a private detective.

There was a response to the message... a response signed by Lito Russo, CFO of AC Tech and Security.

Fucking hell. That must be the Lito that Wendy was talking to.

There was a photo of him attached to the signature of the email. He was a handsome guy with dark, close-cropped hair, a strong nose and brow, and light brown eyes. His arms were crossed against his chest, which gave his biceps a bit of a pump. There was a black-and-white octopus tattoo on his forearm, the tentacles seeming to wrap around his wrist.

I looked up at the group, some of them already seeming to grow impatient with the silence. "Sorry, the Bluetooth is having trouble connecting," I called out as I clicked into the "recently deleted" folder. This was likely where I'd find an even larger golden nugget, but I was also running out of time. The second I pressed Play on the music would be the second I lost my reason for sitting there and snooping through Archie's laptop.

My eyes jumped from subject line to subject line. All of it appeared to be spam, a string of incoherent words advertising local singles and miracle sex pills. I was about to close out of it and go back to the group when something jumped out at me. It was an email address, one I recognized:

WhosEatingTheRich.com.

That was from the blogger who had written the story on Amelia's death. The one who knew about the secret nanny camera, who must have had an inside connection to the family.

There it was. An email coming from Archie's business account, detailing all the facts of the case that had been missing from public record. He'd been the leak. But why? Did he know something that he didn't even tell the blogger? Was he laying the groundwork for some kind of plan I couldn't quite figure out? Did he just want to get the word out that something was fishy with his mother's death?

So many questions and absolutely zero time to figure them out. Archie was walking in my direction, the rest of the group already standing on either side of the field with their respective teams. I clicked out of the web browser, but not before spotting an email welcoming Archie to an online gambling website, and opened Spotify just as Archie came to sit next to me.

I clicked Play, and the music started, loud and heavy with bass. "Look at that," I said, standing up. "You're a good-luck charm."

"Guess so," he said, glancing at the laptop before looking back up at me. I motioned toward the team.

"Ready to play?" I asked.

"Yeah, I just remembered I have to send an email real quick. You guys can start without me."

"Sounds good," I said, turning to join my team. Playing flag football was the last thing on my mind.

27

COLTON COOPER

THERE WERE plenty of reasons why I found Eric sexy. His wit and charm were up there, along with his permanent five-o'clock shadow and his dark hair that always felt like silk in my hands. I also loved how he could make me laugh with the dumbest joke, and some of them were *really* dumb, but he would tell them with full conviction and have me rolling on the floor because of it.

But there was one thing above all else I found sexy about Eric: how fucking good he was at his job. Maybe it was because I came from such a career-driven family, but having a skill and a passion to use it really turned me on.

So you could imagine how damn horny I was when Eric filled me in on what he was really doing with Archie's laptop.

We had finished our field day and were back in our bedroom, my team taking the trophy (and the $250 Amazon gift cards that came along with it, one for each of us). It had been a fun time without any dramatic blowups, which surprised me. It also reminded me of a time when our family was whole and happy together. It had been a rare occasion and only happened in my early childhood, but they were warm memories nonetheless, and having a little piece of that back felt good.

"Hey, Colt, have you seen my wallet?" Eric asked as he buttoned the last button on his collared shirt. We were getting ready for the second portion of today's events: the murder-mystery dinner. A little too on the nose for my liking, but I was gay—it's literally written into the code of my DNA to never say no to a themed dinner party.

"Wasn't it on the dresser?"

"That's usually where I put it, yeah... oh, weird. Here it is. On the windowsill." Eric walked over to the window and grabbed his wallet. He looked like a full-on five-course meal, wearing a sexy pair of black Calvin Klein briefs and the white collared shirt, with tall socks that went up to his calf.

"Anyways," Eric said, grabbing the pants from the ironing board and tugging them on. "I want to figure out why Wendy is saying 'I love you' to her husband's CFO and why Archie is speaking to journalists about what happened."

I nodded, bringing my focus back to the matter at hand. "And we're sure it was Lito on the phone?"

"I've got it recorded. That's who she was talking to."

"This is such a mess," I said, sitting on the edge of the bed. I'd gotten a little further than Eric, already wearing my slacks and formal navy blue dress shirt, the sleeves rolled up. It had been Jen's idea to have us all dressed up like we were attending a gala, and it was always hard saying no to her. Besides, I didn't mind dressing up every now and then. Especially not when I was doing it with a man that looked like Prince Charming mixed with Ricky Martin and a little bit of classic James Dean flair. He was a gentleman that could turn into a wolf at any moment, and that drew me to him like a moth to a burning hot flame.

"Oh, hold on... Tristan says he might have found something."

"What? What is it?"

"He says he needs a little more time but that he might have a video from the nanny cam."

My heart leapt to my throat. "Eric, if he gets video from that night—it might be all we need. We could end up knowing what happened to my mom before the night's over."

He nodded, sitting down on the bed next to me. He put a hand on my leg. "Whatever happens, just know that I'm here for you, okay? I've got your back."

"Thank you, Eric. None of this would be happening if you weren't here. I owe a lot to you." I put my head on his shoulder, that overwhelming sense of being home flooding through me. Like stepping back into your grandma's house after a few months of being away and smelling the same sweet aromas from the fresh bread she used to love to bake.

"You don't owe me anything. You'll never owe me anything. Whatever I do for you has no cost. Absolutely zero."

"Still," I said. "You took a risk in coming along for my crazy plan."

"And it looks like the risk paid off big-time already." Eric leaned in for a kiss. Soft and sweet. It made my pulse quicken as heat rose up to my cheeks, spreading out from my chest.

"It has paid off," I said, looking into his eyes and realizing there was no one else I'd want to be with. Ever. I found bliss inside those soft brown eyes, and I never wanted to be without them again.

"I love you, Eric." The words fell from my lips, colliding with him, his eyes opening wide for a moment before he smiled.

"I love you, too, Colt. You're my other half. Always have been, always will be." He kissed me again, lips still curved into a smile against mine. I felt like we'd been launched into the stratosphere. I couldn't get higher if I tried. Hell, smoking an entire blunt wouldn't get me as high as I felt in that moment. I'd been wanting to hear those words from Eric for years now, ever since I'd fallen asleep in his arms, back when I'd just turned twenty, new to feeling those intense emotions and scared to admit to them. I'd kept it to myself back then, realizing it was all too soon, but I knew it even back then: I was in love with Eric Ruiz, and I could say it out loud now.

We managed to break through the spell and finished getting ready without any further distractions. I wasn't all that excited about the night, especially not when all I wanted to do was sit Archie and Wendy down for an hours-long interrogation session. Something was up with them, and I wanted to figure out what.

"Just absorb every little detail," Eric told me as he walked through the wide hallway toward the dining room. "Even the small things could end up being way more important than you think."

"I thought I gave this investigative life up when I dropped out of the academy."

"I'm glad you didn't. I need a Watson by my side."

I chuckled at that, squeezing his hand in mine. "Do you think they actually fucked?"

"Oh, for sure. Or at least touched tips."

That got a belly laugh out of me.

"The tips of their magnifying glasses?" I asked.

"No, the tips of their co—hi, Jen!" We had just turned a corner and nearly walked right into my sister. She was wearing a white dress that dripped in jewels down to her ankles, clinking and sparkling as she took a couple of steps back, her red-bottomed heels catching my eye.

"Well, don't you look like an absolute icon," I said, snapping my fingers in the air as she gave a twirl. Her hair fell down past her shoulders in sleek brown waves, shifting with the light as she turned back to us.

"Thank you, thank you. Both of you cleaned up really well, too. Excited for tonight's murder-mystery dinner?"

We both nodded in unison. Macy and Luna came down the stairs at that moment, Macy in a sharp ever-green blazer and pants and Luna in a more modest green dress with a white shawl over her shoulders. "I heard there's a mystery to solve?" Macy said, giving Jen a side hug.

Good thing we've got a detective here tonight, huh?

I followed my family through the living room, chatting with Luna and Eric about Luna's newest addition to the family: a tiny calico kitten named Marbles. Luna managed to show us about four hundred and fifty photos of Marbles before we made it to the dining room, where the rest of the family was already gathered. My dad sat at the head of the table, with Jax sitting at the furthest spot from him. Kendall scrolled through her phone as if she was already bored with tonight's event.

"The last of our guests," my dad said, clapping his hands together. He looked a little stressed but well put together, his suit thrown over the back of his chair. He wore a blue-and-pink polka-dotted bow tie, which I thought was an interesting choice.

Eric and I took our seats at the long dining table. There were already delicious-looking appetizers placed throughout—tiny stacked cheeseburgers, garlic and parmesan peppers in a savory ponzu sauce, a bowl of escargots— along with champagne glasses filled to the brim for every person. Two large bouquets of roses and lavender gave the table an impressive height, as if the flowers were reaching up to touch the chandelier that hung from the ceiling. A couple of floor-to-ceiling windows looked out at the scenic French Alps off in the far distance, painted yellow and purple by the setting sun.

It was the perfect setting for what would end up being an absolute train wreck of a night.

"Alright, well, we all know Mom loved these kinds of games," Jen said, standing up and moving a strand of hair from her face. Or was she brushing away a tear? "And since this trip is mostly in her memory, I thought it would be great if we could dress up and honor her by being the family unit she knew and loved. I wish she could be here to play with us, but I'm sure she's looking down at us right now, ready to yell at Colton for missing the most obvious clues."

I laughed along with the rest of the table. I did tend to be the most oblivious sibling, although tonight, I was determined to keep my focus sharp. It was why I kept glancing toward Archie and Wendy, who were both extra quiet tonight. Wendy sat with her back straight and her body angled slightly away from Archie. It was the complete opposite of the body language between my other brother, Matt, and Krystine, who were clinging to each other like they were about to float off into the sea together.

Jen went on to explain the rules of the night, the lights going off just as she finished. A shriek followed, the lights coming back on to reveal one of the housekeepers lying on the floor, fake blood oozing from underneath her. A fake knife rested next to her, along with a note. Jen got up and grabbed the note right when Eric's phone buzzed. I noticed his attention shift down to his lap, where I glanced to see a video playing on his screen. I immediately recognized my mom's living room, clear as day.

Time froze. Even though Jen was still speaking, I couldn't make out a single word she was saying. I had to look away. If I witnessed my mom's murder, I would end up vomiting all over the table. I gripped Eric's leg, trying to stop the world from spinning.

"Okay," Jen said, taking her seat. "So let's start with questions. We can have a big roundtable type of interrogation session while we eat our salads and then break off into smaller groups. That sound good?"

"Jen, you seem awfully in control of all this," Matt said suspiciously, a hand on his chin. "Almost like you orchestrated the murder yourself."

Jen rolled her eyes. "Matt, I have a clear alibi. I was at work at the time of the murder. Check the fact sheet that's under your plate."

Matt moved his plate and read over the sheet, eyebrow still arched. Jen continued on, but all I could keep thinking about was the video that had landed on Eric's phone.

"Alright, so who's got a good question we should start with?" Jen said, a notepad open next to her Caesar salad.

"Eric, you should know," Kendall said, narrowing her lids so that her gaze took the sharpness of a knife. "You're the private detective, after all. Is that why you're here? Faking your relationship with Colton?"

What in the actual fuck?

Kendall had clearly woken up today and chosen violence.

I looked at her, shocked, before my head swiveled to Eric, who cleared his throat and sat back in his chair.

How did she know any of that? And why was she bringing it up now? Kendall and I were never close, so I didn't expect a private heart-to-heart conversation, but she was still my sister. I *did* expect some kind of compassion from her.

That's when Eric further sent me into a state of shock. "You're right," he said. "It's all true, but I'm not here to investigate a fake death. I'm here looking into a real one. The murder of your mother."

What? What the hell was going on? Had mercury suddenly slipped into a severe retrograde? Did some swamp witch just pull out a voodoo doll and turn me upside down?

Eric's hand on my thigh started to move. A single finger tracing shapes—no, letters. He was writing a message on my leg. *Lay the bong?* He used his palm to motion wiping the slate before tracing the letters one last time... *Play along.*

"Colton... seriously?" Jen looked shocked, her eyes bouncing between us. She seemed hurt. "Fake?"

I nodded, unable to form words past the knot in my throat.

"You know what? To hell with all of this." My father stood so fast from his chair that it tipped over, crashing onto the floor. Macy jumped in her seat with a shout, covering her mouth with her frail hands. "Jackson, grab the will. We're reading it now and ending this fucking trip."

"But, Dad, wait, " I said, wanting to give Eric time to

work. He had all the pieces; now he just needed to put them together.

"No. This ends now." My father stormed off into the living room. Kendall sat back with her arms crossed, a cocky grin on her face as she watched the place burn from the firestorm of chaos she'd started.

I could only imagine this night getting a whole lot worse before it got even a tiny bit better.

28

ERIC RUIZ

I KNEW WHO KILLED AMELIA. It was right there on my phone. A video that showed a masked assailant sneaking up behind Colton's mom and wrapping a rope tight around her neck, dropping her to her knees and squeezing until the life left her body. The assailant was covered in black from head to toe, even wearing gloves to hide their hands. I made sure no one could see my phone as I watched it one more time just as the chaos started to erupt around me.

There were two distinctive details that immediately caught my eye. One was the golden chain the assailant wore, left clearly visible against his dark shirt. It was a necklace I was sure I'd seen before.

The other detail that struck me happened toward the very end of the short video, where the killer's sleeve shifted for a brief moment, allowing me to see what appeared to be a feather tattoo on the person's wrist.

I looked across from me, at Archie, my eyes dropping

to the golden chain with the same initials that were attached to the chain in the video. Archie didn't have any visible tattoos, but could that be because he was covering them with makeup? Or maybe the tattoo in the video was a fake to throw off investigators?

"Jackson, the will." William was livid, standing behind the tall love seat, his fingers digging into the upholstered fabric as his eyes raked across the gathered group. We had all moved to the living room, where the walls felt like they were slowly inching toward us.

Jackson sat down on the couch, lifting a briefcase and setting it on the coffee table. He moved aside the glass vase holding some bright red roses and undid the lock to the briefcase. He clicked it open and lifted the case as if a snake was going to launch out of it and bite him. I looked to Archie, who was biting his nails, Wendy sitting down next to him as they both crammed into the other love seat.

Your own mother.

Archie's face started to morph, teeth growing sharp, nose turning hooked, ears growing into horns. All features I thought he shared with Colton, now they all resembled some kind of demon, crawling up from the ground to take whatever he wanted, no matter the cost.

Colton's hand found mine. An idea was forming in my head, but it would require some light acting from the two of us. I had to get a confession from Archie before the night was over, and I think I knew how to do that.

I took a step forward. "Before we read the will, I think we should talk about who stands to gain the most from it," I said, my gaze floating across the room before landing on Archie. "Because that's the person who I believe killed Amelia."

There was a collective gasp from the room. There. I lit the fire; now I just had to make sure I didn't get burned. "What the hell are you talking about?" William asked me, face turning firehouse red.

I glanced at Colton. This next part would be difficult but necessary. "You all know me as Colton's boyfriend, but that's not how I started this trip off as. I came here because Colton hired me to do a job, to investigate Amelia's murder and get to the bottom of what happened."

Kendall scoffed, rolling her eyes. "I fucking knew something was up."

William looked to his son, eyes wide. "Colt, is that true?"

"It is," Colton said. Jen sucked in a sharp inhale. "I felt like something was wrong with how Mom died, and so I asked Eric if he could help."

"I came as Colton's fake boyfriend so I could investigate without raising any suspicions. At first, I wasn't entirely convinced someone here was involved, but then the pieces started falling into place, and my mind changed."

"This is bullshit," Matthew said, grabbing Krystine around the waist and walking them toward the exit. "Email me with whatever I get in the will. I'm out of here."

"Matthew, sit." William's eyes captured the intensity of a thousand burning suns. Matt looked like he was going to argue but swallowed his words and moved to the couch in silence. Tensions were clearly high, but that was fine. I found that dropping my suspects into a stressful pressure cooker of a situation usually extracted the truth from them. "What did you find?" Colton's dad asked, those fiery orbs turning to me and nearly reducing me to a pile of ash right where I stood.

"I found that one of your sons has all the reason in the world to benefit from a large sum of money landing in his lap."

All eyes in the room turned to Matt before some jumped to Archie. No one suspected Colton.

"This is *sooo* much bullshit," Wendy said, chiming in. "You're full of bullshit, just like the relationship between you and Colton. I had a feeling there was something going on, something weird. I decided to check it out myself, finding your wallet, googling your last name—see, I can be a detective, too. I found out you have your own private-eye agency in Atlanta, so of course I knew you were a fraud." She was clearly drunk with the way some of her words slurred, the glass of champagne in her hand likely her fifth by now.

"You found my wallet, or you dug around my room for it?"

"Doesn't matter," she said, looking indignant. "What matters is that you're a phony and a fraud, and you shouldn't even be on this trip."

"Let him speak," William shouted, his "dad" voice in full effect. Everyone in the room seemed to shrink down by a couple of inches. Except for me. I took center stage, feeling a familiar rush of adrenaline that followed the successful closing of every case.

"At first, Amelia's death was described as a botched robbery, but there were a few big question marks that kept me thinking there was something else to it: first off, only a few pieces of jewelry were stolen. Yes, someone can argue that the burglar got scared after her death and only took a couple of things, but this person had to have known Amelia would be home because this person knew to go exactly when the cameras would be down.

"But not *all* the cameras were recovered from the scene of the crime. There was a nanny cam that had been taken. A nanny cam that was installed by a familiar tech company: AC Tech and Security."

Archie's eyes opened wide, Wendy's jaw dropping. Archie stood, shaking his head, getting paler by the second. "No, I didn't do it. I didn't install any nanny cams in Mom's house."

"It was a good thing you installed them," I continued on, ignoring Archie. "Since you desperately needed the job. Now that your gambling addiction has kicked back in and you owe the bank something close to two hundred thousand dollars."

Archie sputtered some incoherent words. Colton stood next to me, his face expressionless to anyone who didn't know him like I did. But I'd spent hours and hours staring at that face, admiring every tiny move, every blink, every twitch. I could see he was in pain, and a lot of that pain was being inflicted by the revelations I was dropping. Should I have debriefed him before? If I knew this would be how the night went, I would have sat him down and told him everything I discovered—but there was no time.

"You'd go to your wife for help, but she's been distracted lately, hasn't she? It seems like your own CFO is the one distracting her, too. But you already knew that, didn't you? You already felt like life broke you down once before; you weren't going to let it do it to you again." I took a step forward, keeping unwavering eye contact with Archie as I spoke my next words. "That's why you killed Amelia."

Wendy gave a shrill shout, and the glass of champagne she'd been holding twirled to the floor and shattered against the polished marble, bubbly gold spreading over the veiny white. Silence followed as everyone in the room absorbed the accusation, shock spreading like sarin gas through the air.

Archie spoke first, his voice hoarse, a hand against his throat as if he was having trouble breathing. "I didn't do it. I didn't kill my mother."

His denial sounded sincere, but the evidence sounded more convincing. I looked to William, his eyes drilling a hole through his son. He had taken off his suit and unbuttoned the first three buttons on his shirt, as if his clothes were becoming too tight. I understood the signs of a panic attack. I had to end this as quickly as I could. I needed to get Archie to confess.

Which meant increasing the pressure.

Before I could speak, Archie stomped toward me and nearly knocked Wendy from her chair. Rage filled the space, coming at me like a tidal wave. "You don't even belong here on this trip. You and Colton concocted this entire plan to, what, frame me? Do you want me off the will, Colton? More money for you and your fake boyfriend? Huh? Eric, do you get a cut?"

He spoke out of anger, like a rabid dog barking and snarling after being pushed to the corner. It meant I'd got him; I just had to push a little further. I had to apply the pressure.

"Eric and I—"

I jumped in. "Colton brought me here as a detective, first and foremost. Yes. Our relationship was fake, but the information I uncovered is all real, and I wouldn't have found any of it if I didn't act the part with Colt." It may have come out a little harsher than intended, but I needed to keep an air of authority, and stressing my place here as a detective came before clarifying my place here as Colton's boyfriend. I could tell it hurt Colton. He likely expected me to stress that we weren't fake—that we were never *actually* fake. But I couldn't, not now. Not when I had Archie exactly where I wanted him.

That's when Kendall got to her feet, shooting up from her chair like a bolt of crimson lightning, her strapless skintight dress showing her phoenix tattoo, splattered with pastel watercolors. "This is fucking crazy. We're standing here, dressed like fucking Clue characters, talking about Archie like he could hurt a fly, much less our own *mother*. Do you see how ridiculous that sounds?"

The tattoo... Archie has none.

Still, I had to push ahead. Maybe the answer was closer than I thought.

I took out my phone and opened it to the video. Archie tried snatching it out of my hands, asking me what it was.

"It's proof of your involvement in Amelia's death." I turned to Colton, who hadn't left my side this entire time. Except now I wasn't so sure I wanted him to stay. Not for this.

"Do you want to stay here for this?" I asked him. He answered with a solemn nod.

I pressed Play, and the family gathered around, except for Macy and Luna, who stood at the far end of the room, looking absolutely horrified. We watched as the masked figure came up behind Amelia's unsuspecting figure and strangled her from behind with a rope.

Colton turned away, Matt stumbled backward, and Krystine started to cry.

Archie and Wendy looked closer at the video before Kendall spoke, throwing another wrench into my theory. "That's not Archie. He was Mom's same height—that person is clearly much taller than her. Look."

"But how does he have your necklace?" William asked, gaze falling to the very necklace Archie was now wearing.

He thumbed it, shaking his head. "I don't know. I had lost it for a few months. I found it in my underwear drawer, but maybe someone had it?"

I looked down at Archie's wrist. No tattoos, but could

he have had temporary ones placed just for the crime? Could he have thought that far ahead?

No, that didn't seem right... there was something I was missing. I looked at the video again, pausing it on the frame that clearly showed the tattoo. It didn't look fake. It looked slightly faded and—holy shit. That wasn't a feather.

I was wrong. Archie didn't kill Amelia, but now I was sure I knew who did.

29

COLTON COOPER

I COULDN'T BELIEVE any of this was happening. My entire world felt flipped upside down. Yes, when I'd bumped into Eric at the coffee shop, I knew that asking him to solve this could very well implicate someone in my family, but... my own brother? The same one I'd walk to the playground with after school? The same brother who would sit on the couch with Mom and watch old *I Love Lucy* episodes together? Archie had his problems, but I always considered him family at the end of the day—how?

I didn't look at the video. Couldn't bring myself to watch. I instead watched Wendy, who had her back against the wall and her arms clutching herself tightly. She wore a black dress that shimmered with every tiny movement she made, giving away the fact that she was trembling.

That's when Kendall pointed out the height difference between Archie and the killer. Wendy's shaking became more intense, her shoulders looking like they wanted to fall right off. I cocked my head, turning my gaze back to Eric. He held everyone's attention as he scrubbed through the video.

He looked up, first at me, then at Archie, then finally at Wendy. He stopped the video and put the phone back in his pocket.

"I'm so sorry, Archie. I was wrong. I misread some of the evidence."

"Seriously?" Archie said, anger still flushing his face a bright pink.

"I'm genuinely sorry. But I wasn't that far off, actually."

I cocked my head. "What do you mean?"

His eyes seemed to be locked on Wendy while her gaze appeared to be locked on the floor. Why did she seem so nervous? What the hell was going on?

"I thought that the video proved Archie was there, but I was wrong. The video was meant to *look* like Archie was there, wasn't it, Wendy?"

All eyes turned to Wendy, who still wouldn't look up.

"What the hell are you talking about?" Archie asked. I looked to my father, who was watching this all in a simmering silence, his fists tight at his side.

"I thought the person in the video was you because of the necklace and because you'd know where the camera was installed. But I was wrong—you wouldn't know there was a nanny camera because you weren't the one who installed it, were you? That would have been Wendy, who I'm assuming makes house calls whenever a client's important to you, am I correct?"

Archie blinked as if trying to regain his vision after a flash grenade. "I, uh, yeah, that's right, but..."

"And the months you lost your necklace are likely during the same time your mother died. The same time the necklace appears in that video, on a man who's taller than you and who happens to have a tattoo on their arm. A black-and-white tattoo of an octopus, with the tentacles wrapping around the wrist. Sound familiar to you?"

I watched as the pieces started to fall in place, my brother shaking his head and looking to his wife. "Lito?"

She finally tore her gaze up from the floor. Her eyes were full of unshed tears, her bottom lip quivering. "I'm so sorry. It was his idea, Archie. Please, you have to believe me. It was all Lito's idea."

"You did it? You killed my mother?" It was like flipping a switch inside a pitch-black room. Light flooded the space, shining on the cold and merciless truth.

"I didn't—it was Lito. He's right there on the camera."

"But you were with him every step of the way, weren't you, Wendy? You knew to take the camera, you knew to give Lito your husband's necklace, you knew that the mountain of debt you two were piled under would be a great motive to pin the murder on Archie. So you took the nanny cam, and you emailed a blogger, leaking information to set up a narrative. One you could use to land your husband in jail, which would leave you and Lito free to enjoy whatever spoils Amelia left in the will."

My jaw dropped. Wendy's tears flowed freely now.

She looked like a shadow trying to press herself back into the wall. It was her. She had orchestrated my mother's death, all so that she could run off with the bag and her side guy, leaving my brother framed and behind bars.

An unfiltered, raw, and *crimson* kind of rage started to fill me. I wanted to throw myself across the room, shout at her, ask her how she could be so monstrous. I wanted to cry and fall to the ground. I wanted my mom back. I'd never be able to hug her, or hear her voice, or laugh at her jokes, or reminisce about a childhood story, or— "You fucking bitch." The words flew out of me like daggers. I'd never called a woman that, not in the manner I just used, not with the aggression that fueled my never-ending well of pain. "How could you?"

Kendall was on Wendy before anyone could blink. She had a fistful of Wendy's hair. Jen screamed for her to stop, grabbing at our sister's elbow but getting thrown backward. Jackson tried to intervene, but it wasn't until my father stepped in that they were able to pry Kendall off a still-crying Wendy.

An arm settled on my lower back. I turned to look into Eric's worried eyes, and I started to cry, my head falling on his chest, his shirt soaking up the tears. He wrapped me into a tight hug, and for a moment, I felt like everything would be alright.

"You did good, Colt." Eric kissed the top of my head. Wendy was shouting, my grandma was crying, and Krystine and Matt both had to leave the room. It was complete and utter chaos, but being in Eric's embrace provided a bit of a shield. "You recognized something was off and weren't scared to ask for help."

I put my ear to his chest, hearing the thump of his rapidly beating heart. Archie was on the phone, a hand on the back of his neck as he looked at his wife the same way a stranger would look at someone trying to rob them. I didn't realize until a couple of minutes later that Archie had been on the phone with the police.

Wendy knew the gig was up. She collapsed to the ground, her head in her hands as sobs racked her body. She kept saying she was sorry and that it was all Lito's idea, but no one paid any attention, her pleas falling on deaf ears. My grandmother looked like she was ready to strangle Wendy herself. It was Luna who convinced her to leave the room, sensing that the anger in my grandmother's eyes was seconds away from erupting.

Jen came over to my side, so I was flanked by two of the people I cared about the most in this world. I controlled my emotions and stiffened my upper lip, holding Eric's hand in mine as blue light from the police cars outside flooded through the arching windows. The veil of anger started to lift. "You okay?" Jen asked.

"I am. You?"

She nodded, her mascara having run down her cheeks in dark trails of black. She likely wasn't planning on needing waterproof makeup tonight.

"I can't believe she was responsible for Mom's death." Jen's glare could slice through concrete. The police were let in by Archie, who stood aside as they went for his wife, still crying into her open hands. They were gentle with her as she tried to stand and collapsed back down onto the ground.

"We'll read the will tomorrow," my dad said, sounding bone-tired. He grabbed his suit from the back of the chair and walked toward the hall, the suit dragging on the ground from a loose grip.

"You know what's sad?" Jackson spoke up as Wendy was being led out of the room, before she was out of earshot. He and Kendall were standing by the fireplace, the view of the French Alps behind them. "Wendy wasn't even in the will. In fact, there's a stipulation that she wasn't to get any of the money if she and Archie were to divorce before Amelia's death. Fuck, Archie wasn't even getting any money. She didn't want to tempt his gambling addiction, so she left his for charity, leaving him items that were more sentimental in value than actually valuable."

Kendall chuckled before clapping her hands and calling out into the room, "I knew it. She's laughing up at us from hell."

Eric looked at me, confused. "Hell?"

"Kendall thinks everyone's going to hell. Hopefully she's wrong about that." I reached for Eric's hand, resting my head against his chest again, taking in a deep breath. His oaky scent helped calm some of the stormy seas of anxiety that roiled around in my chest. This night was a living fucking nightmare, but at least it was a nightmare that appeared to be ending. It would take some time to fully process the bombshells that were dropped on us tonight, but at the very least, I was grateful to *finally* have some answers. My mom could rest in peace, and the people responsible for her death could be punished. That's all I really wanted.

And it was thanks to the man currently at my side, the only person capable of making me smile in the midst of all this chaos. I looked into his warm brown eyes and felt at home, at peace. It was all worth it.

"Come on," I said, tugging Eric's hand. "Let's go to bed and watch silly TikToks until we fall asleep."

"Yes, please. I've got some new Terri Joe videos I wanted to show you anyway."

I chuckled, exhaustion slipping in past the waning adrenaline. "Good. I need to laugh before I start crying again."

"Sooo... you two aren't fake boyfriends?" Jen asked, finger wagging between the two of us.

"No," we both answered in unison. My sister seemed relieved. I looped an arm around Eric's waist and dropped my head on his shoulder. "We're as real as it gets," I said. "Now, let me call the American police so Lito can spend the night in jail while we spend it cuddling together."

30

ERIC RUIZ

I FINGERED my fourth Jell-O shot of the night, separating it from the plastic cup and sucking it right into my mouth. The book club cheered, Tristan standing up from Colton's cloud sofa and grabbing the empty tray so that he could refill it. Steven asked for a blue one, while Noah leaned into Jake with his eyes slightly crossed. "Guys, I think Colton's game is easily the most drunk I've ever gotten," he said, shutting his eyes and rubbing the bridge of his nose.

"I warned you," Colton said, grinning as he sat cross-legged on the gray chair, flanked by Yvette and Tia. His oversized T-shirt was from an Imagine Dragons concert I'd gone to. I didn't mind at all that he wore my clothes; in fact, I liked it. I was finding that the longer I spent with Colton, the more I realized that the man could do absolutely no wrong.

Tonight, it was his turn to host the book club. We'd

been back from France for nearly a month now. It wasn't entirely sunshine and roses when we got back. Although we had figured out what happened to Colton's mom, the fact of the matter was that it didn't bring her back, and nothing ever would. That weighed heavily on Colt, especially now that he was looking ahead to a trial after Wendy and Lito had lawyered up. Their defense was nonexistent, but it was now something else we had to deal with.

Still, every day I woke up next to Colton proved to be better than the last, and he felt the same. Soon, a few weeks had passed, and the two of us fell into an exciting and shiny new rhythm. Being official boyfriends meant doing the silly things and getting butterflies from them—holding hands in a group setting, kissing each other good night, waking each other up with morning blowjobs, cooking dinners together, and watching dumb movies where plot wasn't important and evening blowjobs took center stage.

Every day, I learned something new about him, too. Like how he had a talent to spell anything backward or how he had a deathly fear of kangaroos. Random things I wouldn't have known about him if I wasn't living with him, spending these moments discovering those hidden gems that made up who he was as a person.

"Nico, is this what you expected when I told you about Reading Under the Rainbow?" Jess asked, a hand on Tia's thigh. Nico Martinez was Jess's cousin and another Atlanta transplant who was looking for some sense of community. He was a quiet guy with longer hair and arms full of black-and-white tattoos, and he always had a smile on, no matter how many Jell-O shots he'd already had.

"Not at all, no," he said, pushing a strand of thick jet-black hair from his eyes. "Not at all."

"It's probably the best book club you've ever been a part of, though, right?" Tristan asked, his expression clear that he expected one answer and one answer only.

"Yes, it is."

"Ding, ding, ding," Tristan said, placing a tray of colorful Jell-O down on the table. We got back into our discussion on the book, having just reached the end of it this week and figuring out who had murdered the grandmother.

"I still can't believe it was Alecia," Yvette said, shaking her head so that her mane of curls caught the light. "Her own granddaughter? That's cold, man."

"And for what?" Jake asked. "She thought she was going to get the property, which would have given her access to the gold that was buried there. Instead, she got part of the pig pen and a couple hundred dollars. The grandmother definitely got the last laugh there."

"What did you just say?" Colton asked.

"Ah, shit," Jake said, realizing his mistake a moment too late. "Is 'laugh' a trigger word?"

"No, but 'grandmother' is. Take your pick," Colton said, motioning toward the tray of shots. He had come up with a game called Jell-O Land Mines, where certain words would trigger an "explosion." Only he knew the list, but that didn't stop him from drinking since he'd occasionally trigger an accidental explosion himself.

Jake grabbed a blue one and shot it back. We continued our meeting well past ten o'clock, but none of us cared. We were having way too much fun being together again.

Slowly, people started to trickle out until it was just Colton and me left, slightly drunk and still giddy from all the laughter.

"Well, that was a fun night," I said as Colton closed the door on the last of our guests. He walked over to me, smiling, his hands landing on my hips.

"It was. It feels good to be back with everyone instead of on Zoom."

"I'm glad we're growing, too. At this rate, we're going to be a full-on nonprofit organization soon."

Colton cocked his head. His eyes caught the light in a way that instantly cast a spell on me. I couldn't ever get enough of that handsome face, especially not when it was so close to mine. "Can we maybe do a for-profit organization instead?" Colton asked. "And then we can branch off into charity."

I chuckled, kissing the tip of Colton's nose.

"What was that for?" he asked, his face scrunching up in slight confusion.

"For being perfect in every single way. For never holding grudges. For proving to me that love is real and second chances are deserved." I kissed him again, this time on the lips. His tongue slipped into my mouth, his taste flooding through me. A taste that had me addicted from the first hit. Colton's hands moved under my shirt, rubbing my lower back as the kiss intensified.

"You proved to me that second chances are worth it," Colton said, his voice low, his breath tickling my lips. The fire in my core lit to a roaring flame. I shifted my hips forward, wanting Colton to feel what he was doing to me. The khaki shorts I wore did absolutely nothing to hide how hard I was becoming.

"There were so many ways our lives could have turned out. I could have driven past that coffee shop. You could have decided to move somewhere else. I could have refused to go to France with you. But instead, everything fell exactly into place, making this moment right here possible. Making us possible." I kissed him again, holding him tighter against me. He was hard, too, his length throbbing against mine.

"Come," Colton said, a hand on my chest, his hips flush against mine. "Let's see what else is possible between us." He leaned in and bit my bottom lip, pulling a moan from me as he turned and led us to the bedroom. I took my shorts off in the hall, Colton grinning as he walked with my cock in his hand, as if he were steering me forward. I couldn't help but smile, feeling so natural and comfortable with this man. I used to have a difficult time being fully intimate with someone, always wondering if they were judging the fact that I didn't have a six-pack or a defined chest. Gay men could be assholes about body types—that wasn't news to anyone—but I *never* felt uncomfortable around Colton. Not once. He always looked at my body in a way that made it feel as if he were worshipping me. I never had to second-guess his attraction for me, and that made me all kinds of horny.

Colton and I finished ripping off our clothes once we got to the bedroom, falling onto the bed with Colton underneath me, his hard cock rubbing against mine as we kissed. I could feel a streak of precum wet my belly as Colton rutted his hips up, moaning into my neck. He reached for my ass, squeezing and kneading as I ground my cock down against him, our bodies writhing in pleasure that was unmatched.

"God, I fucking love you so much, Colt." I kissed him again, sucking on his bottom lip. My balls tightened, and my body lit up with a jolt of electricity as his finger slipped into my crack.

"Oh yeah?" Colton said, looking up at me with a smolder in his gaze that rivaled the heat of the sun. "Show me how much you love me."

I licked my lips, smiling as I moved off the bed so I could kneel on the floor, Colton's feet on either side of me. I picked his leg up, took off his sock, and started massaging the sole of his foot before I sucked his toe into my mouth. He moaned, dropping back on the bed. I kissed the sole of his foot, moving up to his ankle, up his calf, watching as his cock throbbed. He was as hard as a brick, pointed straight up at the ceiling.

He placed both hands at the base of his cock and gave it a shake. He had the most photogenic fucking dick I'd ever seen. It was about seven inches, uncut, with a juicy thickness to it. He was shaved down to a dark-haired stubbled, his balls smooth and relaxed between his legs.

I buried my face in them, sniffing his scent and wishing I could bottle it up. I looked up at him, smiling as he slapped his cock against my cheek. I kissed his shaft, licking the head, tasting his precum before I sucked him into my mouth. He groaned, the sound of his pleasure dumping gasoline onto the hungry inferno inside my core. I swallowed him down to the root, catching his eyes as they rolled back into his head with bliss.

I worked on giving him the best damn blowjob of his life, starting off slow, tracing lines up and down his shaft with my tongue before I deep-throated him again. I made him nice and wet, letting him stay in my throat as I gagged around his size, locking eyes so that the connection between us thrummed with intensity. I wanted all of him, but not just in my mouth. I wanted something else, something I hadn't done in a while.

"Colt, I want you to fuck me tonight."

His eyebrows jerked up in surprise before his grin cocked into that of a hungry wolf. "You just had to ask." His cock pulsed in my grip. I licked the droplet of precum that leaked from the tip. I had played with my ass and bottomed for the guy I was with before Colton, but it wasn't something the two of us had done, and I was ready to change that. I wanted him on top of me, thrusting into me, opening me up with his thick cock.

I leaned over and opened the drawer in the night-stand, grabbing the slick bottle of lube. My heart was racing but not because of nerves. I was excited. I wanted to share this with Colton. Give him my body in a way that not many others had had.

I wanted to ride Colton into a blissed-out eternity, and that's exactly what I planned to do tonight.

Well, that and one other thing.

31

COLTON COOPER

RAIN PATTERED GENTLY against the window. The only light in my bedroom came from two lamps on either side of the bed, washing the space in a warm glow. Eric lay on the bed, holding his legs up and lifting his ass in the air. I took a moment to admire him, to really drink in the sight.

Eric was my everything. He wasn't only perfect in the physical sense, but he also completed me in an emotional sense, too. I didn't think I could have gotten through these last few weeks if it hadn't been for Eric staying at my side, keeping my spirits lifted and my thoughts from spiraling. He was a constantly reassuring force, one I'd never take for granted. I'd lost him once already, and I was determined to never let that happen again.

"Fucking hell, how are you so sexy?" I asked, lining my lubed-up cock with Eric's tight hole. He lifted higher off the bed, giving me more access. His soft eyes slowly shut as I pushed in.

"Is that okay?" I asked, holding his legs as the head of my cock was enveloped by an intense heat. I was filled with an urge to thrust forward, to bury myself balls-deep inside of Eric, to become one with the man I loved beyond anything else in this world.

But I didn't have to be an experienced top to know that would be a bad idea. I took him exactly how I wanted to be taken, gentle and slow at first before changing gears.

"*Whoa*, go a little slower," Eric said, his eyes opening wide as I sunk in another inch. I listened to what he said, rubbing his chest and stomach and pulling slightly out before trying to go any deeper. Part of me was nervous. I didn't want to hurt him. I knew I was thicker than average, but I rarely ever topped, so I wasn't entirely sure just how to handle it.

Still, the bliss that came from being inside Eric was hot enough to burn away any anxiety. Eric completely trusted me, and I trusted him, meaning as long as we kept an open line of communication between us, nothing could go wrong.

I tried to sink in a little deeper. Eric's mouth turned to the shape of an O, and I paused.

"Keep going," he said. He reached down and grabbed his tight balls in one hand and started stroking himself with the other. I watched myself disappear inside his hole as his body relaxed enough to fully let me in. We both let out deep, chesty groans as our bodies became one. I leaned down and kissed him, wanting this man to know just how fucking much I loved him. I didn't want to share this moment with anyone else in the world.

"You're everything to me," I said, whispering the words against his lips. I slowly pulled back before sliding back in all the way. He gasped, his half-lidded eyes showing just how dick-drunk he'd started to become. I was used to the flipped view, where I'd look up as Eric plowed me into kingdom *come*, but I had to admit, seeing Eric give me those puppy-dog eyes and hearing those sounds get pulled from his throat as I stretched him open really was an entirely new level of hot.

Looked like I was going to have to top more often.

I put my fists down on either side of Eric and hitched his legs up on my shoulders. "That okay?"

He looked up at me and nodded, giving me the green light. I started to slide in and out of him, fucking him harder and harder. Eric started to grunt with every thrust, his eyes rolling back in pure pleasure as I rocked my hips into him. He looked deep into my eyes, his gaze pleading for more. His hands on my shoulders tightened their grip, his nails beginning to bite into my skin. I thrust harder, spurred by the gasps Eric let out.

Sweat beaded on my forehead, dripped down my chest. I was consumed by the flames. Eric moaned, the sound mixing with the rhythmic slapping of skin against skin. I continued to buck into him. Faster. Harder. Deeper.

More, more, *more.*

Eric's eyes shut, his hand gripping his cock. His toes

curled in the air. He tried to warn me, but the words wouldn't form. Instead, the first sign I got of his orgasm was the way his hole convulsed around me, tightening and pulling me in deeper. He shot his load moments after, cum coating his hairy chest and belly. His hole continued to spasm, even as I fucked the last drop of cum out of him.

My climax wasn't far behind. I thrust one last time, burying myself down to my balls as I collapsed on top of him, my arms giving out as I filled him with my load. I nuzzled my face into the crook of his neck, moaning with every shot, my legs stretching out behind me. It was ecstasy in a way I couldn't even begin to describe. Rainbows and butterflies and pots of gold erupted all around us. The bed formed a cloud, and the moon served as a spotlight, shining down on the two of us.

"Holy shit," I said into Eric's neck, my breaths coming in fast. "Wow."

"Yeah, you took the words right out of my mouth." He chuckled, his chest rising and falling with the sound. I slowly pulled myself out of him, a squelch sound making us both chuckle. I kissed his chin, his cheek, his lips, smiling as I lay down on the bed next to him, a leg tossed over his, my swollen and slick cock pressing against Eric's thigh.

"Now I see why tops have it so easy. They don't have to prep, *and* they get to feel that good? Who do I have to write a letter of complaint to?" I joked.

"I'm not sure. Ru Paul? Cher? The HRC?"

"Hillary Rodham Clinton?"

"No, the Human Rights Campaign."

I nodded before I started to laugh, both of us cracking up, our bodies floating on a river of pure bliss. I didn't want this night to end. After everything we'd been through, after getting a taste of how boring and empty my life felt without Eric, I knew that moments like these had to be cherished. I had to tuck this night away into the "unforgettable" file.

Little did I know, it was about to become a whole lot more memorable.

"It's raining," Eric said, looking out the window. Our bedroom faced out to the yard, which was currently in bloom with all the spring flowers I had planted. A wall of purple lavender hugged the fence that surrounded the property, washed in the light of the brightest full moon I'd ever seen, fighting through the sparse clouds that seemed intent on keeping the drizzle going. We planted it to remind us of our time in France.

"Come," Eric said, getting off the bed and heading toward the bathroom. "Let's clean up and go outside for a second."

"Outside?" I asked, arching a brow. "Why don't we stay inside and go for round two?" I rebutted.

"Because I want to dance in the rain with you."

I cocked my head. Eric had shown spurts of romance before, but this was the most romantic thing I'd ever heard him want to do. I smiled, getting up and following him into the bathroom, where we took a couple of quick bird baths before we each pulled on a pair of house shorts. Eric had to get something from the room—I figured he wanted to film this since he had gotten pretty deep into filmmaking lately. I had a sneaking suspicion he was making some kind of movie about us, but I wasn't entirely sure.

He met me at the sliding glass door that led into the yard. It wasn't a heavy rain, but still enough to soak the concrete around the pool and turn it a dark gray. I looked at Eric, seeing the same kid I'd fallen in love with on that first day in the academy. The one I'd stayed up all night watching *South Park* with, wondering if one of us would ever make a move.

I grabbed his hand, and we both stepped out, barefoot, the rain falling down in soft sheets. I laughed, feeling like the magic in the moment far outweighed the absurdity in it. Eric opened his phone, but instead of filming, he pressed Play on a song and set it down on the covered patio before coming back to my side. He took my hand in his, placed another on my hip, and we started to dance. It was likely terrible and would make a professional choreographer want to rip their hair out, but to me, it was perfect.

It was midnights like this that made me believe in love. I looked into Eric's eyes, rain dripping down his face, over his lip. I brushed some of it off his cheek, resting my hand there. "I love you so much, Eric."

"I love you, too, Colt. With every fiber of my being." Raindrops wet his long eyelashes. I kissed him again, tasting the rain on his lips. He wrapped me up in a tight embrace, our dancing turning into a slow two-step, moving side to side, feeling the rhythm of the music blend with the beat of the falling rain. It was a storybook moment, and I couldn't imagine sharing it with a better person.

The dance slowed, and Eric took a step back, gaze locked on me, his fingers slipping through mine. "You're my one, Colton. I know it now, I knew it then, I'll know it for the rest of time. I feel like I'm myself with you, and that's rare to find, even rarer to find it twice. But I did." He let go of my hands and reached into his pocket. That's when he started to drop to one knee, and everything clicked into place with the intensity of a roaring freight train.

Holy crap, he's proposing, oh my dear gay god in heaven, he's proposing.

"Colton, you complete me in ways I didn't even know I needed. You make me a better person every day, just by wanting to be better for you. In the grand scheme of things, I know we've been together a relatively short amount of time, but that doesn't stop me from wanting to spend the rest of my life with you. So, Colton Jimmy Dean Rogers Cooper, will you marry me?"

He opened the black velvet case to reveal a glittering silver band set in a silky blue pillow. I surprised myself by laughing *and* crying at the same time, something I didn't realize was possible until that very moment. I nodded, moving the hand from my mouth so Eric could hear my answer clearly. "Yes, absolutely fucking yes, I'll marry you. *Yes.*"

Eric slipped the ring onto my finger and stood up, his

grin reaching from ear to ear and lighting up his entire face.

"Also, my grandma would be impressed with your middle-name game."

"Thanks. Thought of them on the spot."

I shook my head, smiling, kissing him, my man—my fiancé. Holy shit. We were getting married.

"You're the best," I said, unable to keep my lips off him, the rain beginning to stop as the thick gray clouds moved away and let the full moon shine bright in the sky.

"Come on," Eric said, tugging me toward the house. "You said something about a round two?"

"And three and four. This ring is doing something to my libido."

"Wait until you see the other ring I got you, then," he said with a wink and a laugh. I wasn't sure if he was serious, but I didn't care, having already gotten the only ring I cared about. I followed him all the way back to the bedroom, where we fell into bed and didn't get out of it until well past noon the next day, having only gotten a total of four hours of sleep and still waking up bright-eyed and bushy-tailed.

Guess that was an effect of waking up next to the love of your life and soon-to-be husband.

EPILOGUE

Tristan

ERIC AND COLTON looked the happiest I'd ever seen them. When my best friend FaceTimed me a couple of months ago, I was expecting the worst. My brain was a trap of pessimism and anxiety, with slight dashes of impressive creativity, which meant that I sometimes thought up the worst situations possible: car crash, helicopter crash into an active volcano, eaten whole by a whale shark. I flashed through all kinds of reasons why my best friend would be randomly FaceTiming me before I accepted the call and was greeted with two beaming faces on the screen.

Of course they were calling to tell me the news of their engagement.

I couldn't be happier for them. Eric had talked to me about Colton on a couple of different occasions, before they had bumped into each other at the coffee shop, always mentioning him in a way that made me think he was Eric's "one that got away." Thankfully, life had other plans for them.

Now we were in Disney World, celebrating the couple at the happiest place on Earth with all our closest friends. The entire book club was here, all of us wearing shirts with Eric and Colton's faces printed onto them. Noah had made them before the trip, insisting that we all had to wear them, even though it was supposed to be upward of a hundred degrees by lunchtime, and Noah hadn't exactly splurged on the most breathable fabrics.

Still, we were all having a blast, even if I had to take the shirt off and tie it around my waist. Sweat was already soaking through my black tank top, which made the Mickey Mouse Popsicle I was currently sucking on all the more necessary. I sat on a bench outside of the exit for Space Mountain, Jess and I waiting for the gang to get off the ride since neither of us did roller coasters.

"Jesus Christ, it's hotter than a blacksmith's ballsack out here."

I looked to Jess, my eyebrows raised.

"Sorry, I've been reading a lot of fantasy books lately."

We both started to laugh. "No, you're completely right. I think that's a better comparison than I could have come up with, and I'm the writer of the group."

"You should take it," Jess said, taking a long chug of her soda. "But credit me, or I'll sue the absolute crap out of you."

I chuckled, nodding. "You'll be the only citation in

the entire book. A tiny footnote after 'hotter than a black-smith's ballsack' credited to Jessica Martinez."

"That's all I ask for." She winked and started to laugh while fanning herself with a folded-up map. The sun beat down with relentless force on the crowded park. Families lined up to take a walk under the misters; others gathered underneath palm trees and awnings just outside of the shops and restaurants, where random drafts of AC-blasted air would sometimes flow. A little girl dressed like Elsa twirled her way past us in her blue dress, completely oblivious to the heat that was slowly draining the life out of her parents.

My phone buzzed in my pocket, making my heart buzz against my ribs with the same vibration. Every message I got lately kicked off a flight-or-fight response in me, ever since I'd attracted the attention of some creep on Tinder. It started off innocently enough, and the guy seemed like boyfriend potential. After a years-long dry spell, this die-hard romantic was thirsty for any kind of relationship—fling, boyfriend, shotgun husband, what-ever kind of dick came along, I was looking to ride it.

Well, as one can imagine, that life motto led to a lowering of standards, which then led to connecting with a man who did not take no for an answer. I'd never even met the guy in person, deciding to cancel our first date after I got some sketchy vibes from a phone call we'd had. It wasn't anything major, just my gut telling me to call things off. And yes, I was as thirsty as a bass in the desert, but I wasn't ready to throw it all away because of that.

So I canceled our date, only to receive a string of threatening messages telling me I'd regret it if I didn't show up. They were unsettling enough for me to block and report the guy, figuring that would be enough.

It wasn't. He found me on each of my social media profiles and continued to message me, telling me how quickly he had fallen for me and how badly he wanted to meet me. He promised me a life full of yacht parties and champagne showers and wild, hot sex lasting all through the night.

Little did he know I hated all of that. Well, not the last part. I loved sex, but I couldn't give a piss about someone's money. Of course, I wouldn't expect this guy to know that about me after a couple of days' worth of texts between us. And vice versa. All I knew about him was that he collected clown fish and lived in Atlanta, and that's really all I wanted to know.

And yet I continued to get messages. He'd make new accounts after I blocked the old ones, and the messages started getting darker. I wasn't easily spooked, but this guy was making me look over my shoulder every now and then.

Thankfully, the number on my phone wasn't my obsessed admirer. It was the detective agency that I'd hired to stop him.

"Sorry, Jess, I gotta take this call."

"Go for it," she said, sitting back and scrolling through her phone.

"Hello?"

"Hi, Tristan. This is Zane with Stonewall Investigations. How are you?"

I took a bite of the vanilla chocolate Popsicle, the cold ice cream giving me momentary relief now that I was out from underneath the umbrella. "I'm doing well. Just celebrating a friends' engagement here at Disney."

"Congrats to them. My family actually has a trip booked to Disney next month. My daughter's more excited about that than she was for Christmas." I heard some papers being shuffled in the background, along with the sound of a dog barking in the distance. "I don't want to spoil your trip by any means, but I do think it's urgent we talk about your case."

"That's okay. Today's our last day, so any bad news won't be all that bad."

"Okay, because unfortunately, I do have some bad news. But first, I want to assure you that I'm putting all of Stonewall's resources behind you. In fact, I'm assigning you someone from our Elite division. They handle our more involved cases."

I cocked my head at that. "Involved? What makes my case so involved that you have to call in the big guns?"

"Well, Tristan, we aren't one hundred percent certain, but we're starting to believe this man you were talking to is actually the serial killer known as the Midnight Chemist."

The world seemed to have been sucked into a black hole. Everything went silent, even though children were still laughing and rides were still roaring and parents were still chatting. Eric and Colton walked out of the exit, holding hands, Eric's hair messed up from the ride, the rest of the group right behind them. My knees felt like they'd been replaced with sponges, and my legs started to shake.

"What?" Eric asked as he walked over to me. "It looks like you just saw a ghost?"

Yeah. I did see a ghost.

And that ghost was me.

———

Receive access to a bundle of my **free stories** by signing up for my newsletter!

Tap here to sign up for my newsletter.

BE sure to connect with me on Instagram and TikTok **@maxwalkerwrites.**

WANT MORE MAX? Join Max After Dark.

AND IF YOU enjoyed this story, please consider leaving a rating or review! They help immensely in sharing this book with others.

Max Walker
Max@MaxWalkerWrites.com

ACKNOWLEDGMENTS

Thank you, Camille, for creating another illustrated cover pulled directly from my wildest dreams!

Sandra, your a word-wizard and my books would look far different without you.

Vania, again you slayed my time-line demons. Thank you!

Armando, to a lifetime of midnights like these.

And thank you, reader, for going all the way to France with my boys. Let's see where life takes us next.

ALSO BY MAX WALKER

Book Club Boys

Love and Monsters

Midnights Like This

The Stonewall Investigation Series

A Hard Call

A Lethal Love

A Tangled Truth

A Lover's Game

The Stonewall Investigation- Miami Series

Bad Idea

Lie With Me

His First Surrender

The Stonewall Investigation- Blue Creek Series

Love Me Again

Ride the Wreck

Whatever It Takes

The Rainbow's Seven -Duology

The Sunset Job

The Hammerhead Heist

The Gold Brothers

Hummingbird Heartbreak

Velvet Midnight

Heart of Summer

Audiobooks:

Find them all on Audible.

Christmas Stories:

Daddy Kissing Santa Claus

Daddy, It's Cold Outside

Deck the Halls

Printed in Great Britain
by Amazon